Adam
&
Evelyn
Pat Ballard

PEARLSONG PRESS
NASHVILLE, TN

Pearlsong Press
P.O. Box 58065
Nashville, TN 37205
http://www.pearlsong.com
http://www.pearlsongpress.com

Cover & book design by Zelda Pudding

Original trade paperback ISBN 978-1-59719-081-7
Ebook ISBN 978-1-59719-082-4

ALSO BY PAT BALLARD
ASAP Nanny | Dangerous Love | The Best Man | Abigail's Revenge
A Worthy Heir | His Brother's Child | Nobody's Perfect | Wanted: One Groom
Dangerous Curves Ahead | 10 Steps to Loving Your Body
Something to Think About

Library of Congress Cataloging-in-Publication Data

Ballard, Pat (Patricia F.)
   Adam & Evelyn / Pat Ballard.
      pages ; cm
   ISBN 978-1-59719-081-7 (softcover : acid-free paper) — ISBN 978-1-
59719-082-4 (ebook)
   1. Mothers and daughters—Fiction. 2. Women—Violence against—
Fiction. 3. Clergy—Tennessee—Nashville—Fiction. I. Title. II. Title:
Adam and Evelyn.
   PS3552.A4664A64 2015
   813'.54—dc23
                                        2014043386

Praise for Pat Ballard & Her Books

"Good messages about body image and integrity
without getting preachy. All around fun read."
JGIRLSMEME about *Dangerous Love*

"...charming, witty and tender love story with a twist."
MIDWEST BOOK REVIEW about *Nobody's Perfect*

"I just wanted to let you know that your books
have changed my life in a matter of days...
In the last 2 days I have read *Nobody's Perfect* (1st),
Dangerous Curves Ahead (2nd), *A Worthy Heir* (3rd),
His Brother's Child (4th) and just finished *Abigail's Revenge*.
They were all awesome....I have been overweight
my entire life; I never thought that I was pretty—
my husband tells me that I am, BUT until I read
your books—WOW, I am telling you, life changing....
God Bless you always!"
TERESA S

"Ballard's easy-to-read, easy-to-use volume is like having
your own personal coach and cheerleader for
ending the warfare and making peace with the body
you have...*10 Steps* is your body's best friend in pocket form."
SUSAN SCHULHERR
author of *Eating Disorders for Dummies*

CHAPTER 1

A LATE SEPTEMBER WIND BUFFETED HER CAR AS EVELYN Carmichael exited I-65 and headed into Nashville, TN. She'd never been to Nashville. In fact, she'd never been this far north. But it seemed like a long way from south Mississippi, and she wanted to be a long way from south Mississippi. From Meridian, in particular.

The only reason she'd picked Nashville was because it was a large city, and she hoped that she could hide from Darren Carmichael if he decided to look for her. She could have stopped in Birmingham, which she had driven through, but that was too close to Meridian. Only one hundred and fifty miles away. To her it made sense that a smaller city would be the first place Darren would look. But she hoped he'd try Jackson, which was in the opposite direction than she'd taken.

Nashville was around three hundred and thirty miles from Meridian, and Darren would never believe that Evelyn had the courage to drive that far on her own. Little did he know what desperation could do for a person.

No, Darren wouldn't follow her to Nashville. She hoped he didn't care where she was, as long as she was away from him.

Plus, Darren couldn't give a flip about country music. He

was from a long line of old money and family who loved to flaunt that old money. He was all about the country club scene and putting on good appearances that included a big house, a fancy car, and a fashionably slim wife. And while Evelyn didn't mind a big house and a nice car, the one thing she wasn't was slim.

Genetics hadn't handed Evelyn the "slim card," and after making it painfully clear to Darren that she was finished starving herself to try and obtain the size he wanted his wife to be, the verbal and mental abuse had started.

He hadn't tried to hide the fact that he'd had affairs with other women. In fact, he'd deliberately left evidence everywhere of what he was doing. And when she'd questioned him about it, he'd admitted it and said she could leave—but that he'd have her arrested for kidnapping if she tried to take Annabel, their four-year-old daughter, out of the state.

Not that he loved Annabel. He'd resented "that baby" from the moment Evelyn told him she was pregnant. Evelyn had hoped that once he saw the baby after it was born he would warm up to it, but he'd been cold and distant to the child, even though little Anna constantly tried to get her father's attention. It seemed that the more she vied for his attention, the more he pushed her away.

Darren hadn't made any attempt to save their seven-year marriage, so Evelyn filed for divorce, he paid for it, and with less hassle than it took for them to get married they were divorced. And here Evelyn was, headed as far away from her home state as she thought she needed to go.

Evelyn's heart hurt to know that Anna was still in Mississippi with her mom, but for now that's how it had to be. If she tried to take Anna out of the state, Darren Carmichael would do everything he could to make her life miserable, even if it meant using their beautiful little girl to do it.

It was late September, and she wondered if she'd be able to

make it back to Meridian in time for Thanksgiving. It made her terribly sad to think about having to miss one single holiday with her child.

FROM HIS VANTAGE POINT on the stage Adam Singletary's body went very still as he watched the woman slip quietly, otherwise unnoticed, into the back of the church and take a seat on the last row. She set her purse on the floor and then looked up directly into his eyes. An arc of unseen electricity connected them, jolting his body to the center of his being. *She's finally here*, he thought.

Unnerved and shaken, Adam had enough awareness to realize the choir had stopped singing and the song leader was saying, "And now, here's Pastor Adam Singletary."

As he arranged his notes, Adam noticed the slight trembling of his hands and sent up a quick prayer that he could pull himself together enough to get through his sermon, which today, oddly enough, was about love and marriage.

EVELYN CARMICHAEL felt ill at ease and conspicuous as she slipped through the door of Grace For All Church and took a seat on the back row. Being new in town, she didn't know anyone, so she figured that attending a church was the best way to meet people. And if she wanted to be totally honest with herself, it might help build business in the small dress shop she'd just opened. The latter wasn't the best reason to go to church, she admitted.

After setting her purse on the floor, she looked up into the eyes of the most electrifying man she'd ever come in contact with. Dynamic. That was the word that seared her brain as their eyes met and held. For the first time in her life she understood—no, *experienced*—the word "magnetism." She could see the green flash of his eyes from this distance. Eyes that sparkled like dewdrops reflecting early sunlight on a clear, cold morning. Eyes that held hers with awareness and recognition. But she didn't know him, so how could he recognize her?

Surprise washed through her when the song leader introduced him as the pastor. Up until then she hadn't had time to wonder who he was, but the *pastor?* She'd never met a preacher that affected her like this! In fact, she wasn't even sure she should sit in church with the feelings that were pulsing through her veins.

His short, light brown—probably blond in the sun—hair curled just enough to keep it from spiking from the styling gel he'd used on it. His jaw was square enough to look strong without being stubborn. She guessed he was around six feet tall, with a body that looked fit without being too muscle-bound. He really knew how to make a suit look fine!

He was talking about marriage, she thought. She was sure that he directed most of his message to her, but she couldn't hear what he was saying because of the loud buzzing in her ears from her rampant, very non-churchy thoughts.

She had to get out of here! Coming here was an obvious mistake. As soon as the closing prayer started she quietly took her purse and headed for the back door, keeping her head down in what she hoped was a prayerful position.

And ran right into the disquieting pastor, who had just arrived at the back of the room to greet the congregation as they left.

"Was it something I said?" he teased, as his hands clasped her shoulders to steady their jolting bodies.

"I'm sorry. I have to go," she whispered in a husky voice, as the deacon finished his closing prayer with a strong "AMEN!"

"Wait! Don't go. I want to meet you. Officially," Adam called. But she was already halfway down the long steps that led to the parking lot.

"Who is that woman?" he asked the first person who came through the door to shake his hand.

"That's the woman who just opened The Woman's Boutique, just off of Harding Place. I believe her name is Evelyn Carmichael," answered Sally Johnson, the church's official gatekeeper. Normally one would have called her a gossip, but everyone knew that gossiping was wrong.

"Ahhh," Adam whispered. "I believe I have finally met my Eve."

MONDAY MORNING, as soon as Adam thought the store would be open, he walked casually through the door of The Woman's Boutique. A soft tone from over the doorway sounded his entrance.

"I'll be with you in a moment," a melodic voice came from a back room.

He recognized the voice from the brief meeting at church yesterday. Her voice had a lilt to it, as if she were about to break into laughter or song, he wasn't sure which. But one thing he was sure of—he wasn't imagining it yesterday when that voice made all the nerve endings in his body tingle.

All of his adult life Adam had been haunted by the scripture in Genesis that said that it's not good that man should be alone.

Or, as his mom used to say when she'd get exasperated about his dirty room, "Oh, it is *not good* that man should be alone!"

At 37 years old, he'd begun to wonder if he would spend the rest of his life alone. He'd tried to convince himself that he could learn to love some of the women he'd met along the way. He'd sure had enough matchmakers in his congregations through the years. But none of the women had been what he was looking for. Not one of them had ever felt right to him. He knew exactly what he was looking for in a woman, and he was sure that he'd recognize her when she came along.

He'd often wondered if maybe he should just settle for some good Christian woman and forget about his "dream girl." But he knew what he wanted, and wasn't willing to settle for less just so he could say he was married.

Right now, listening to the echo of her voice ring through his head, he was very happy that he'd held out. She had come, just like he knew she would.

So what will you do if she's married? A little voice in his head whispered. "For a preacher, you sure do hear lot of voices!" Adam scolded his unwelcome reminder.

"Excuse me?"

The pleasant voice at his elbow wasn't in his head.

"Did you say you hear voices?" A smile tried to break away from the corners of her mouth.

"Well," he grinned, "that's just a matter of speech for this irritating little voice of reason that's always mouthing off in my head."

She was even more striking than he remembered from his brief encounter the day before. As the morning sun filtered in through the window, her dark brown hair sparkled with red highlights and exploded in unruly curls around her face. Large amber eyes watched him with guarded amusement.

"Is there anything in particular that you're looking for, Pastor?" Now the smile broke through like a beam from oncoming headlights as she indicated the room full of feminine clothes that hung or lay folded. "Maybe something for your wife?"

Adam had never seen a smile that startled him before, but hers did. He took a moment to regain his composure before saying, "Please call me Adam. I'm Adam Singletary. I dropped by to officially meet you, since you hurried past me too quickly to do so yesterday. And I'm not married." *Can you get anymore stilted?* he wondered.

"I'm Evelyn Carmichael," she stated simply, and held out her hand.

"Hello, Eve," he said, taking her soft hand in his and holding it just a little longer than necessary.

"Evelyn," she repeated, pulling her hand from his, uncomfortable with the shot of awareness that tingled its way up her arm. "I like to be called Evelyn, if you don't mind." Actually, all her family called her Eve, but being Eve to his Adam felt just a little too awkward.

"Are you married?" Adam asked.

"Divorced."

"Well, I want to say I'm sorry, but under the circumstances my conscience won't let me lie."

"What circumstances?" Evelyn was beginning to feel slightly uncomfortable.

"I'm attracted to you, so if you were married I'd have to ignore my feelings. Wanna go to lunch?" The quick grin flashed at her.

"Well. Wow. Do all ministers move this fast?"

"It's really not that fast. I'm 37, and I've waited a long time for you."

"Whoa! Wait just a minute. You're weirding me out. You don't know anything about me."

"Okay. I'm just a little nervous, so I guess I'm acting like a teenage boy, but I would like to have lunch or dinner with you and find out more about you. And if you twist my arm, I'll tell you a few things about myself."

Charm cloaked him like a fine linen suit. And again, Evelyn felt a slight niggle of uneasiness. Just because he was the pastor of a church didn't make him automatically a saint. Maybe he was a wolf in sheep's clothing.

As the musical doorbell announced the arrival of someone Adam said, "Look, I'll go visit the sick and comfort the troubled like a good pastor, but I'll drop back by at noon, and if you want to have lunch with me we can walk across the street to The Lunch Box and share some stories. I mean, it's not a date, it's just lunch. But if by noon you still don't want to have lunch, then I'll ask you again tomorrow."

As he walked from the store Evelyn stared at him with a half-open mouth.

"Isn't he just a doll?" Julie Walker, the young woman who had just come in and who helped Evelyn in the store, said with awe and admiration in her voice.

"Julie! Is it proper to say something like that about your pastor?"

"Well, why not? I mean, yummy is yummy. I don't care what title he wears!"

Her logic quelled any questions that Evelyn may have proposed.

"And he wants to take you to lunch!" Julie continued. "Now that news will cover the congregation quickly—Pastor Adam never, and I mean never *ever* dates! And every person who knows an eligible female has tried to set him up. My mom tried to set me up with him when he first moved here several years ago, but I was totally in love with Jim, so that didn't work. Not that I thought it would have, anyway. He's yummy to look at, but he's just not my type. Too smooth. I like my men kind of rough around the edges, like Jim."

Jim was a mechanic at the Ford dealership, and loved to hunt any animal or bird that was in season.

"So, are you going?" Julie asked without taking much of a breath.

"I don't know. Is he, you know, normal?" Evelyn asked, causing Julie to break out in a peal of laughter that caused a passerby on the sidewalk to glance toward the window.

"What on Earth are you talking about?" she asked.

"Is a preacher supposed to ask a total stranger for a date? Isn't there some kind of religious rule against that?"

"Ministers are just men. They have the same feelings that any normal man has. So if he's attracted to you, why shouldn't he ask you for a date? Maybe he has an extra ability to sense your spirit and knows you're okay."

"I don't know. He just acts different than any minister I've ever been around."

"Have you ever been around a young, single minister who loves life and enjoys it to the max?" Julie asked.

"No."

"Well, there you go,'" Julie said, and proceeded to go to the back room to put her lunch in the fridge.

"'Well, there you go?" Evelyn said as she raised her hands in the air. "As if that settles the whole thing!"

As Adam parked his car and headed to The Woman's Boutique, he sent up a prayer that he wouldn't make a fool of himself and totally turn Eve off. He realized everyone didn't understand his off-handed sense of humor, but it was such a part of him that it was unnatural to try to curb it. But, he reminded himself, there's a time and place for everything.

He glanced at his watch as the musical door chimes announced his arrival. High noon, and he felt as if he was about to be in a shoot-out. No woman had ever made him this nervous. This had to be a good thing, didn't it?

"Come in," Julie said, smiling at Adam with a special twinkle in her eyes. "How may I help you, Pastor Adam?"

"From that mischievous look on your face, I think you already know how you may help me, Julie Walker," Adam said, feeling suddenly a little insecure and embarrassed.

"EVE!" she called. "Your lunch date is here!" The quiet giggle that followed indicated that she knew how impish she was being.

Evelyn came through the door of the adjoining room, which served as the office and storeroom, with a slight frown on her face. "Julie, I haven't lost my hearing! You don't have to let half the town know my business." But as she glanced around and saw that there were no other customers in the store, she visibly relaxed.

13

So he wasn't the only one who was nervous, Adam thought.

"Eve, it's not like this will be a secret after you and Adam have lunch at The Lunch Box," Julie pointed out. "Adam knows that's a very busy place."

"Julie, have you ever thought about getting counseling for talking too much?" Adam asked as he saw realization flood Evelyn's face.

"Oh, please! You two just go and have lunch and forget about everybody else and their wagging tongues."

"She has a point, Eve. If we walk out this door together, tongues will wag. But if you don't walk out this door with me, tongues will start wagging about me spending so much time in a woman's boutique. They might even start to think I'm a cross-dresser!"

This brought another peal of laughter from Julie, and he saw a smile actually trying to crease the corners of Evelyn's eyes.

"On the other hand," he continued, "you could just come over to my place tonight and I could make dinner for you. I don't think too many tongues would wag if I entertained you in the parsonage."

Evelyn turned abruptly and went back into the office.

"Oops! Did I overdo it?" Adam asked Julie while his stomach sank to his ankles.

"I'll go check—" Julie started, but was interrupted by Evelyn bursting back into the store with her purse in her hand.

"I can see I may as well get this over with or I'll never hear the last of it from you two comedians," she said, then poked a finger in Adam's chest as she walked past him. "The name's Evelyn," she said as she went out the door.

Adam winked at Julie and followed Evelyn out. "But Julie called you Eve—why can't I?" he asked as he fell in step beside her. She could walk really fast for a woman who didn't appear to be over 5 foot 7.

"Because she's a friend, and I'm not sure what you are, yet," she hissed, trying to keep her voice from being heard by all the people they passed on the narrow sidewalk. Hopefully the brisk September breeze kept the passersby from hearing what they were saying.

Before Adam could answer they had crossed the street and were walking in the door of The Lunch Box, which was already crowded.

It seemed that half the diners knew Adam and hailed him with greetings, some of which required him to stop and chat for a moment. But after what seemed like an eternity to Evelyn, the hostess finally seated them in a booth in a relatively quiet corner.

Evelyn took a deep breath of relief and tried to hide behind the menu that she had been handed.

"Are you uncomfortable with crowds in general, or just about being seen with me?" Adam asked.

"Both," she answered. "I don't like crowds in general, but especially when I'm with someone everyone knows. Been there, done that," she added, and then wished she could snatch the last part back.

"So your first husband was well-known?"

"I've only had one."

"So far."

This made her lower the menu and look at him. His clear green eyes held hers, daring her to glance away.

"Don't you ever plan on remarrying?" Adam asked innocently.

"No."

"Well, plans have a way of changing on us, don't they?"

His eyes still held hers captive, and she couldn't seem to even blink, much less look away. "Adam—"

"Let's decide what we want to eat," he said, finally glancing down at his menu. "The open-faced roast beef with grilled onions and peppers is really good."

Since that sounded good, Evelyn nodded. "I'll take that and a glass of unsweetened tea," she said.

"Any sides?" he asked.

"No, I'm good with just the sandwich."

The waitress walked up and Adam ordered the same thing for both of them, but added sweet potato fries to go with his.

"So why was your first husband so well-known?" Adam asked, crossing his arms on the table and leaning toward her.

If the back of the booth had allowed her to, Evelyn would have tried to back away from his close proximity. She could almost feel his breath fan her hair, causing tiny sensations to creep up and down her spine.

"You have a one-track mind, don't you?" she said, hoping she could hide the effect he was having on her.

"I'm just making conversation. It was you who mentioned it. Would you rather I talk about how beautiful your hair is when the sun shines on it? Or how your eyes flash with every emotion you feel? Or how kissable your lips are? I'd really enjoy exploring all those topics with you, if you'd rather."

By now, Evelyn's entire body was vacillating between hot and cold.

"Adam! What is wrong with you? You're—"

"I'm a man who is quickly becoming enamored with a woman. Eve, I really hope you're not a Jezebel. I'm in deep trouble if you are."

CHAPTER 2

Evelyn sat in her small apartment in south Nashville and stared at the phone she'd placed back on the receiver.

She had a major problem. Her mom had just found out that she had to have rotator cuff surgery in a week, and couldn't look after Anna until her shoulder was healed. Her mom had injured her rotator cuff about a year ago, and it had never quite healed, but she hadn't expected her mom to have surgery now.

What was she going to do? She didn't dare go back to Meridian to live, and Darren had made it clear he'd take Anna from her if she tried to take her out of state.

But since he hadn't even shown up at the custody hearing, the judge had awarded Evelyn full custody. So how could he get her for kidnapping if she had full custody? Shouldn't she be able to take Anna anywhere she wanted to? There'd been no discussion of where Evelyn could or could not live with Anna.

Plus, if he tried to cause any trouble with her she'd take him to court, because he'd never sent one child support check to Anna. He hadn't wanted to pay child support "for a child he didn't want to start with," as he told the judge. But of course the judge insisted that he did have to pay.

For some reason, in her total belief in Darren's power she'd never questioned what he'd said. And had never considered forcing the child support issue. She just didn't want to have to deal with him on any level.

Well, it was time to start questioning. It was too late today, but tomorrow she'd call her lawyer in Meridian.

Just the possibility of having Anna with her shot a surge of adrenaline through her, and tears rolled down her cheeks.

Suddenly she was filled with ideas about how to fix up the small apartment and make a home for Anna.

THE NEXT DAY, Evelyn's lawyer confirmed that since she had full custody of Anna she could take her anywhere she wanted to.

But she also knew that Darren Carmichael would try to make good his threat if he found out she'd taken Anna out of Mississippi. He'd do it for spite. He'd do it just because he thought he could.

EVELYN GLANCED at the sleeping Anna in her car seat, in the back seat of the car. How did she ever make a child that beautiful? Evelyn wondered. The sunlight reflected off Anna's blonde ringlets, turning them to gold. Even with her eyes closed in sleep, she looked like a clone of Shirley Temple. And Evelyn knew that she'd fight any power to keep her baby.

Darren Carmichael didn't know her very well if he thought he could bully her into giving up her child. She hadn't fought him over the harsh things he'd said and done to her, so he had no idea the side of her that could make his life hell if he pushed her. Only a few people knew that side of her.

She'd driven down to Meridian and stayed with her mom until the surgery was over and her mom was home and settled in. And now she was heading back to Nashville. She'd gotten a later start than she'd wanted, but they should be home before midnight.

Home. As the word slipped so easily into her thinking, she knew that she did feel at home in Nashville. She was coming to realize that Nashville was a large city with a small town feel that she wanted to raise Anna in. There were so many family-type things to do in Nashville. Among many other things there were a lot of parks, and she could see Adam and her taking Anna on picnics, playing in the park—

"Whoa!" she said aloud, and then glanced back to see if Anna still slept. How did Adam slip so quietly into her planning for the future? And why had he?

No! Absolutely not! She simply would not allow another man to come into their lives to jumble the peace that she dreamed of having with Anna. He could take his beautiful green eyes and his charming smile and find some other woman to ensnare. She didn't have time for complications like she knew he could present. Nope, that door was definitely closed. He might be a minister, but he just looked like trouble.

At twenty-eight years old she was more than mature enough to take care of herself. She didn't have to depend on anyone for help.

Her ringing cell phone interrupted her mental tirade. "Hello," she said without looking at the caller ID. It was probably her mom checking on their progress.

"If you're making good time you should be around Birmingham now, according to the time Julie said you left Meridian."

Of all the men she'd met, why did it have to be Adam Singletary's voice that made her go weak all over? Why did his voice have to sound like a smooth caress? She believed he could read the dictionary and it would sound like foreplay! And she just knew she was going straight to hell for having these thoughts about a preacher, for Pete's sake.

"Eve? Are you there? Did I lose you?"

"I'm here," she answered. "I just didn't expect it to be you on the phone. I thought it would be my mom."

"How is she doing?" Genuine concern sounded in his voice.

"She's okay. It's going to take a while and a lot of therapy before she gets the full use of her arm, but she'll make it. She's pretty tough."

"Does she have someone to take care of her until she does?"

"Yes, she has a friend who'll keep close watch over her. And will make sure she's okay." She didn't dare tell him that her mom's friend was male and they had some romantic feelings for each other.

"Why didn't you call me while you were gone?"

"To say what?" He acted like they'd become close friends during the short time they'd known each other.

"Oh, I don't know. Maybe just to let me know you'd arrived okay. Or that your mom was okay. Or that you and Anna had headed home."

There was that "home" word again. And it sounded so right, even coming from Adam's lips.

"Well, I knew you would get all that from Julie, so I didn't think about calling you." Now she was straight-up lying to a minister! He'd been on her mind constantly since she'd left Nashville.

"Liar," his quiet voice said into her ear, startling her. Had she verbalized her thoughts?

"What? What did you call me?" she sputtered.

"Liar. I know you thought of me. I won't believe anything else."

"Adam, we have to talk," she said.

"I know. That's what I want to do. That's why I don't understand why you didn't call me. I wanted to talk."

"About what?"

"What?"

"What did you want to talk to me about?" Her head was beginning to spend.

"Life. Stuff. You know, chitchat."

"Adam, we don't know each other well enough to chit chat."

"Sure we do. A person can chitchat with a stranger."

"Maybe you, but I'm not good at that kind of thing."

"Was the weather good while you were in Meridian?"

"Pretty much normal for this time of year. Maybe a little cooler. The humidity was horrible, as usual."

"Did it rain? It came several thunderstorms here, but nothing major."

"No. No rain this time. But it was windy." What did he care about the weather in Meridian? "Why are you asking about the weather?" she asked.

"We're chitchatting. See, you can do it!"

The laugh erupted from her before she could stifle it. "You are incorrigible," she said.

"That's the first time I ever heard you laugh like that. I really like it. I'll have to be incorrigible more often if it makes you laugh like that."

How was she supposed to respond to that? she wondered. But before she figured it out he continued.

"Eve, I'm falling for you. I just thought I should be upfront about that information."

"No, Adam. No! I can't have that complication in my life right now. I've got to think about getting my apartment set up for Anna. I've got to think about what I'll do when Darren comes after her. I've got to think about how to keep the store above water. I just can't think about how I'm supposed to react to a minister who acts more like a horny teenager!"

Too caught up in her passionate response, she didn't realize what she'd said until his laugh jarred her senses.

"I can't believe I just said that," she said after he'd caught his breath.

"Why not? It was what you thought, so you just said it. And I kind of take it as a compliment, if you want to know the truth. Because that's exactly how I've felt ever since the first time I saw you."

"Mommy," a little voice called from the back seat.

"Anna's waking up, so I need to find a place to stop and let her use the bathroom, and get a bite to eat," Evelyn said, just wanting to be off the phone long enough to find a hole to crawl into.

"Okay, but make sure it's a safe place. And call me when you get back on the road. I'm not comfortable with the two of you being on the interstate this late."

"We'll be fine. I know how to keep us safe."

"Will you call me, please? I don't want to have to worry."

"Okay. I'll call. Bye, now," she said, and disconnected the call. Great! All she needed was some macho man breathing down her throat trying to monitor her every move.

What was she going to do about Adam Singletary?

CHAPTER 3

Evelyn had made better time than she'd expected, and pulled into her small apartment complex a little after eleven o'clock. The first thing that caught her eye was Adam Singletary's late model Ford Flex parked in front of her apartment.

As soon as she pulled in beside him and stopped he climbed out of his car. He was at her door, opening it, before she had time to get her purse and open the door for herself.

"Wow, you made good time, didn't you." He reached for her hand as if to assist her, but she avoided his attempt and stood up. He didn't step back, so she was standing close enough that she could feel the warmth from his body and smell the faint musk of his cologne.

"Why are you here, Adam?" she asked, trying to fight off the warring sensations that coursed through her body. Even in the dimly lit parking lot she could see the flash of green from his eyes. Could see a little puffiness around his eyes, because he'd been asleep while he waited for them.

"I'm here to welcome you home and to make sure you and Anna get inside the apartment okay. This isn't the worst side of town, but this isn't the best side, either. South Nashville has areas that are prone to drug trafficking, and some of the local gangs congregate in those areas. Your apartment is close to some of their activity."

"I'm a big girl, Adam. I can take care of Anna and myself. You're just causing—"

"Mommy?" a little voice inquired from the back seat. "Are we there yet? I need to go potty."

"Yes, we're home, Anna," Evelyn assured her, as she went to the back door to get her.

"If you'll pop the trunk, I'll unload the car," Adam said, standing at the back of the car.

Well, he was here, so she might as well take advantage of it, Evelyn decided, and hit the remote to open the trunk. "There's a good bit," she warned. She'd only brought Anna's clothes and a few extra blankets from her mom's house. She just didn't have the room in the car or her apartment to bring Anna's bed and little chest of drawers. She'd have to worry about that later.

Evelyn gathered the sleepy Anna in her arms and headed for the door. By the time she had it open Adam was behind her with two large suitcases. He followed her in and set the suitcases on the floor. He headed back to the car for the last one, and she headed to the bathroom with Anna.

When Anna had finished going potty Evelyn went back to the living room and found Adam standing there looking around.

"This place is too small for one person, much less a small, active child. You need a larger place so Anna can have some play room."

"Mommy, why is a stranger in our house?" Anna asked, watching Adam as if he were a mass murderer.

"This is our new friend, Mr. Singletary," Evelyn said. "Can you say hello to him?"

"Hello, Mr. Singlehairy," Anna said, and stepped forward to offer her small hand to shake his.

Trying hard to keep the smile from his lips, Adam took her tiny hand in his and, looking deeply into eyes that were so like her mother's, said, "I'm so happy to meet you, Anna. Why don't you just call me Adam? I think that will be much easier to say."

Anna glanced questioningly at her mom.

"I think it will be okay if you call him Adam, honey. Singletary is kind of a hard name for me to say, too."

"I'm glad to meet you too, Adam," Anna said, just before a large yawn escaped from her.

"You two need to get your sleep, so I'll see you tomorrow," Adam said.

"I've got a lot to do tomorrow," Evelyn said. "I've got to get Anna settled in and do some laundry and get some groceries. And I have to call the Tiny Tots Day Care and make sure they remember that Anna has a spot with them on Monday. So you don't need to try to come by."

"Okay. What time are you going to get started?"

"I'm not sure. I'm not on a strict deadline, and I plan to let Anna sleep as long as she needs to. But I'm sure I'll be up by eight."

"Then I'll see you around nine with some breakfast. Want me to bring coffee, too, or do you have coffee?"

"Whoa! Adam, slow down! I said I have a busy day. I didn't invite you to join me in that busy day."

"I know. I invited myself. I'll just come over and then we can make plans for breakfast."

And before she could answer, he was out the door. "Remember to lock this," he said as he pulled it closed behind him.

Did he actually wink at her as he closed the door? Were pastors allowed to wink at women? she wondered as she locked the door behind him.

"Mommy, I'm really, really tired." Anna's small voice

interrupted her thoughts.

"I know, my darling. Come on and I'll show you where our bed is."

"But don't I have my own bed?"

"Not yet. I'll have to buy you a bed, and try to find a place to put it. Our new home is very small."

"I miss my daddy and my big house," Anna whimpered.

Evelyn picked her up and held her tightly as she hurried to the bedroom. The pain in her heart for the hurt that her precious little girl was going through felt like a knife in her chest. Her entire little world had been disrupted, and her normal had become an upheaval.

By the time she'd put Anna on the bed and tucked her in, the child's eyes were already drooping.

Evelyn quickly got ready for bed and slipped in beside her baby. She watched Anna sleep and let the hot, salty tears run down her face. She'd missed Anna so much during the weeks that she'd been with her grandmother. How much longer would she have been able to live without her? she wondered.

She was sorry her mom had to have surgery, but at least that had forced Evelyn to think outside the box that she'd allowed herself to be trapped in and to realize that she needed to talk with her lawyer. It reminded her of the line from the Eagles' song "Already Gone"—*So oftentimes it happens that we live our lives in chains and we never even know we have the key.*

She just hoped her key was strong enough to keep the chains unlocked.

She was about to doze off when Adam Singletary's face popped into her mind and her eyes popped wide open. Speaking of chains. What was she going to do about Adam Singletary? She didn't need another man in her life to complicate things. She didn't care if he was a pastor or an angel from God—if he wore pants, she didn't want him in her life right now.

"Mommy! I'm hungry!" Anna loudly whispered in Evelyn's ear, startling her from the sleep that she'd finally fallen into.

Looking into her baby's precious face the first moment after waking up was the sweetest thing Evelyn could imagine. She glanced at the clock and sat straight up in bed. Nine o'clock on the dot, and as she realized this she heard the loud pounding on the front door.

Adam. Right. On. Time.

Evelyn grabbed her robe and threw it on, knowing that it didn't conceal nearly as much as she needed covered, but she didn't have time to find a better one. Combing her fingers through her hair to try and give it some shape, she called, "Okay! I'm coming!"

As the second round of pounding started up she snatched the door open and almost had a foot land on her shin. There stood Adam, loaded down with a cup carrier with coffee in it in one hand and a large sack in the other one. So he was knocking with the toe of his shoe.

"Sorry, but I thought you might still be asleep," he said as he stepped into the living room and stopped dead in his tracks.

"Here, let me take something," Evelyn said, and took the bag from him. But he just stood and stared at her.

"Okay, I just woke up," Evelyn said, feeling awkward. "Don't say a word about how bad I look."

A slow smile crawled sexually over Adam's face, starting in his eyes and finally making it to his mouth.

"You look warm and soft and sexy," he said. "I should have known you'd look like this when you woke up." And he was having wonderful images of waking up in the bed beside her, but he didn't dare say that.

Blood rushed to Evelyn's face, turning it a dark red. She tried to scold Adam, but no words would form. Her brain seemed to have shut down.

"Good morning, Mr. Singlehairy," Anna spoke from the doorway. "Did you bring food? I'm starving and Mommy slept a long time. I tried to be quiet and not wake her up, but I just got too hungry and had to call her."

The spell was broken, and Evelyn quickly put the sack of McDonald's breakfasts on the table. Then grabbed plates and utensils and put them out.

"Tell me what belongs to who so I can feed this growing child. You shouldn't have brought this. Anna and I could have had cereal until I shop for groceries." She knew she was babbling, but his statement had thrown her so off course she couldn't stop.

Adam put the coffee on the counter and took the sack from Evelyn. Their hands briefly touched, and both felt the effects.

Feeling his eyes on her, but refusing to look at him, she quickly put some food on a plate for Anna, poured her a glass of milk, then said, "Adam, you and Anna go ahead and eat. I need to go and get dressed."

Just then another loud knock came from the front door.

"Are you expecting someone?" Adam and Evelyn chorused together. "No," they both answered.

Evelyn headed toward the door. Not taking time to look through the peephole, she opened it, hoping the storm door was locked.

And she stood looking into the angry blue eyes of Darren Carmichael.

Being too stunned to think of closing the door in his face allowed Darren to reach for the unlocked storm door and push past Evelyn into her small living room.

CHAPTER 4

DARREN STOPPED ABRUPTLY AND TOOK IN THE SIGHT OF Adam, who was now standing protectively close to Evelyn, and Anna sitting at the small dining table eating her breakfast, before his condemning eyes made their way back to Evelyn and took in the skimpy robe she'd thrown on when Adam had knocked on the door.

"So this is how you're raising my daughter? You're shacked up with a man and living in this tiny piece of crap of an apartment?

"You may have made it okay with your lawyer to take Anna out of Mississippi, but I think my lawyer will have a totally different opinion when I explain to him that you're an unfit mother, raising my child in a dump while you're doing the nasty with this loser."

While he'd been talking Anna had jumped down from her chair and run to him, throwing her arms around his legs and shouting, "Daddy! Daddy! You came to see us!"

But Darren Carmichael never once glanced at his excited little daughter. Instead he pushed her tiny arms from around his legs and started toward the door. "I'll see you in court!" His eyes gored Evelyn with contempt, and at that moment she knew that he'd never loved her.

But before Darren could get his hand on the doorknob, Adam grabbed the lapels of his expensive lightweight jacket and shoved him back against the wall.

"Don't you dare come into this house and start threatening my fiancée!" Adam said, holding Darren, a larger man than Adam, against the wall.

The room had gone totally quiet except for Anna's soft sobbing. Evelyn sat on the couch and held Anna closely, but the child still held her hands towards her father as the tears spilled from her eyes.

"Adam, let him go. Please. I don't want this happening in front of Anna," Evelyn said in a soft, even voice.

Adam slowly released Darren and stepped back, fully expecting to be attacked as soon as he did.

But Darren just glared at Evelyn and Anna before turning his hate-filled eyes on Adam. "You will hear from my lawyer. Oh, it's not that I want either one of them," he ground out between clenched teeth. "It's just that I can't stand to lose." He walked out the door.

Suddenly Anna sprang from Evelyn's lap and attacked Adam. "You hurted my daddy!" she screamed, pounding on Adam's legs with tiny fists. "I hate you! Leave me and my mommy alone!"

Adam gently lifted the child into his arms and held her against his chest while she buried her face on his shoulder and wept.

"Fiancée?" Evelyn's voice broke through Anna's sobs.

Sitting on the couch beside Evelyn and shifting Anna to a more comfortable position, Adam said, "Well, I wasn't planning on springing that on you so unexpectedly, but I did come here today with the intention of proposing to you."

Evelyn was aware of his freshly shaven face and the masculine, musky aftershave scent permeating her senses. She was aware of how closely he sat to her, and how gently he held her daughter as her sobs slowly quieted. She was aware of how green his eyes were as he seemed to try to look into her soul. And she was aware of how quickly her heart rate had accelerated.

She rose from the couch and looked down at him, which didn't help at all. It only gave her a better view of him and Anna, who had now curled snugly into his arms and lay looking up at him with all her anger apparently evaporated.

"I'm going to get dressed, and you and I have to have a serious talk," she said, and fled the room.

WHILE WAITING for Evelyn to dress, Adam coaxed Anna into finishing her breakfast. He gathered up the few dishes they'd used and hand-washed them after realizing there was no dishwasher in the apartment.

"What are you doing?" Evelyn asked from the doorway. "You brought breakfast and now you're doing the dishes? Leave those. We've got to talk."

"Anna, I need for you to go to the bedroom and play with your toys so Adam and I can have a grownup talk, okay?"

"But I'm a big girl! I want to hear you talk," Anna said, a mutinous look coming over her face.

"Anna, if you'll go play for a little while and let Mommy and me talk, we'll go to the zoo later," Adam chimed in.

"Really?" Excitement filled the little girl's face. "Promise?"

"I promise."

"Okay. I'll go play, but I can't wait all day, so hurry up!"

"Annabel Renee!" Evelyn scolded as Anna hurried down the hall.

"She's had a hard morning, Eve. Don't be too hard on her." Adam's soothing voice interrupted Evelyn.

"And you!" Evelyn said, turning on Adam and jabbing a finger in his chest. "You will not come into my house and start trying to control everything! How dare you tell Darren that I was your fiancée? And how dare you assume that I would marry you even if you did propose? Are you crazy? For someone who claims to be a man of God, you sure come off as dense!

"And last of all, you do not interrupt and take over when I'm trying to correct my child!" Stopping to take a breath and realizing that Adam had caught her finger, which was rapidly poking his chest, in his hand and held it, she was about to start again when Anna yelled from the bedroom, "I CAN HEAR YOU YELLING, MOMMY!"

Evelyn glanced up and caught Adam trying to keep the laughter held in. "Don't you dare laugh—" But before she could finish she felt laughter bubbling up in her own chest, and couldn't keep it back.

She felt several months of tension draining out of her as she held on to a kitchen chair while she laughed. And the more she laughed, the more Adam laughed. Tears were running down their cheeks when suddenly Anna stuck her head around the kitchen door and said, "That's not talking. That's laughing. I'll *never* make it to the zoo at this rate." And with a disgusted look, she turned and went back to the bedroom.

Finally, taking a napkin from the table and handing one to Adam, Evelyn said, "Okay, let's get this over with," and pulled out a table chair.

"Let me say what's been on my mind for a few days," Adam started. "Just listen and keep an open mind. After I finish, you can ask all the questions you want to ask and I'll answer every one of them. Deal?"

Evelyn only nodded her consent.

Adam poured them fresh cups of coffee, pulled out a chair, and sat down facing Evelyn. "When I moved here, all the married women started trying to set me up with my future wife. I tried to be as patient and kind as I could, but their constant nosing into my life really started to wear my patience out. I finally told them that the woman I loved with all my heart had recently died and I just wasn't ready for a relationship. Now—that wasn't exactly a lie. My grandmother had recently died, and I did love her with all my heart. And that finally got all my eager matchmakers to back off for a while.

"But recently it seems that they've decided my time of mourning has been long enough, and they've started back trying to get me married off." He stopped and sipped on the coffee.

"About five years ago an elderly lady, Lila Smith, an outstanding member of the church, died. She'd been ill for a while, and I used to go to her house at night and read to her, because she had no family. Her husband had been dead for thirty years, and they never had any children. I had no idea about her intentions because we never talked about it, but she left the house to me in her will. And the message along with the house was, 'One day you'll find that perfect young woman that you're waiting for. You'll have children, and you'll need a big house to raise them in. Please accept my house and make it your home and fill it with the children that my Frank and I were never able to have. You're the closest thing to a son I've ever had, and the Lord put it on my heart to leave this home to you. I love you.'

"The house is huge, Eve. I rattle around in it, but I felt like I needed to honor Lila's wishes."

Evelyn started to shake her head in protest, knowing where he was going with this, but he raised his hand and stopped her. "Please let me finish," he said.

"This neighborhood is not safe for a little girl. It wasn't safe for you, but it's really not safe now that you have Anna. There have been drug-related crimes in this apartment complex, and the police have been called out several times.

"You don't have to answer now, but please think about it. It could be in name only until we decided to make it the real thing. It would give you and Anna a safe home in a safe neighborhood.

It would keep the well-meaning church members off of my back. And nothing Darren could do or say could hurt you. I mean, if you're married to a minister, how could he accuse you of being an unfit mother?"

"Is it my turn?" Evelyn asked when Adam paused.

"Yes. Give me your best argument," he said with confidence—but with a sheepish grin, because he knew she was going to hit him with some hard-arguing points.

"First, did you just say that it would be in name only *until* we wanted to change it?"

"Yes. And I mean that. I would never try to force you into a relationship you don't want."

"But you didn't say 'if' or 'until'—you just said 'until.' You seem pretty sure there will be an 'until.' That's kind of presumptuous, don't you think?"

"Not for me, Eve. I've known from the first time I saw you that you're the woman I've been waiting for. I truly believe that I could marry you today and be happy for the rest of my life."

"But you don't know me! How could you possibly say that when you don't know a thing about me?"

"Is that the only thing you're worried about?" he asked.

"NO! I think that Anna can grow to love you in no time flat. Then when it comes time for us to divorce because we finally realize we can't stay together, she's going to be hurt all over again, by another man.

"Then there's the thing that I don't know anything about being a minister's wife! These ladies in your church are going to expect certain things from me, and I don't have a clue what those things will be, much less whether or not I can do them."

"I'll be there to help you, Eve. And there's not that much that will be expected from you. This church has been around for a long time. It has members who have done the same tasks for years and will keep doing them. So there's not really anything for you to do. Actually, a lot of ministers' wives work full-time jobs and just leave the ministering to their husbands.

"Look, let's take Anna to the zoo, and I'll help you do your chores. Just take a few days and think about it. Talk to Julie. She's been going to this church since she was a child.

"Maybe tomorrow, or when you're free, I'll take you and Anna on a tour of the house. I'm really eager for you two to see it."

CHAPTER 5

ANNA'S SOFT, RHYTHMIC BREATHING AS SHE LAY SNUGGLED beside Evelyn was the closest thing to perfection Evelyn could ever imagine. She remembered the lonely nights she'd cried herself to sleep after she'd moved to Tennessee and left Anna back in Mississippi.

But she couldn't quite relax and enjoy the moment. Not after Adam's unexpected proposal this morning, and after the day they'd spent together. What was she supposed to do with the fact that Anna seemed to be totally smitten with Adam and that, just possibly, Adam could be the father figure Anna had craved all of her young life?

And what was she supposed to do about the fact that she desperately needed a larger house and place for Anna to have room to grow and exist in? At this time there was just no way she could afford a larger apartment. She'd tried to figure out a place in this apartment to tuck a bed and spot for Anna, but she didn't have any idea where that would be.

And what was she going to do about the fact that she'd been attracted to Adam Singletary from the first day she'd sat down in the church and met his eyes? She couldn't be around him without being aware of his very presence.

Those green eyes of his could capture her and hold her like a cat charming a bird. And knowing good and well that it was out of line, her fickle heart would jump to rapid rate at the scent of his aftershave, or just being close enough to him to feel the heat from his body.

She'd never felt like that around Darren. Nor any other man. Until Adam, she didn't know what real attraction was. Or was this lust? Whatever it was, it was intoxicating and terrifying at the same time. She wanted more, yet wanted to drive him away as quickly as possible.

By now she had herself worked up into a true state of panic. She quietly threw the covers back and padded to the kitchen to get a drink of water. She had to relax and get some sleep.

As she walked through the living room, she heard voices in the parking lot. She crept to the window and peeked out to see what was happening at 1:30 in the morning.

Two young men were talking, then a small package from one and money from the other one exchanged hands. The one who had received the package got in his car and drove away. The one who had received the money went back into an apartment six doors down from Evelyn's.

Now she knew for a fact that what Adam said was true. There was no doubt that she'd just witnessed a drug deal, and the dealer lived in her apartment complex.

With sudden clarity she knew she would take Adam up on his offer of marriage and a different place to live. She had no idea how it was going to work, but one thing she knew for certain—she'd do whatever it took to protect Anna from being exposed to the kind of danger that lurked in this apartment complex.

With the decision made, Evelyn went back to bed and finally drifted into a restless sleep that was plagued with dreams of human traffickers trying to snatch Anna, drug deals, murders, and a lot of other things in between.

SHE WAS THANKFUL when Anna woke her, leaning on the bed and just staring at her.

"Hi, baby," Evelyn whispered, relieved to know Anna was okay. "Are you ready for breakfast?"

"Uh-huh. I need some egg and toast," Anna answered.

"Well, we'll just take care of that right now."

As they headed to the kitchen they passed through the living room, and Evelyn couldn't resist the need to look out the window and see if the neighborhood looked the same. It did, but the difference was in her mind. She'd gone from feeling okay living here to being downright afraid, overnight.

She made breakfast for her and Anna. As soon as they'd eaten and Anna was playing with her toys, Evelyn dialed Adam's phone. She got his voicemail, so left a message. "It's Eve. Please call me when you can. I saw something in the parking lot last night that has me spooked. I'm ready to see your house and talk about your offer."

While waiting for his return call she cleaned the kitchen and tried to talk herself out of the decision she'd made. Surely there was a way for her to be able to afford a larger apartment in a nicer neighborhood. Maybe if she let Julie go and didn't have any help, she could do it. But no. She couldn't do that to Julie or to herself. If she tried to run the store by herself she'd never have time to spend with Anna.

She knew her mom had money saved, but that was out of the question unless there was some kind of huge emergency.

Someone knocking on the door brought her out of her brooding thoughts. As she stood to go check the door, Anna ran to open it.

"NO! Anna, I've told you to never open the door unless I say it's okay!"

"But you're right there, Mommy. I was just trying to help." Tears sprang to Anna's eyes, and her bottom lip had a slight quiver.

"Baby, I'm sorry I yelled at you, but even if I'm close, we're not allowed to open the door until we look though this little hole and check who it is," Evelyn said, and picked Anna up so she could look though the peephole in the door.

"It's Adam, Mommy! Open the door, it's Adam!"

Evelyn looked through the hole to make sure it was Adam, then opened the door.

"Adam!" Anna yelped, and leaped into his open arms. "You came back again!"

The simplicity of Anna's joy over the unexpected event of Adam coming back again when she'd been used to her own father never coming back hit Evelyn like a ton of bricks. And she knew she was about to make the right decision. If for no one else, this would be right for Anna.

"Hi," she said as he stepped into the room.

Holding Anna perched on his hip with one arm, he wrapped his other arm around Evelyn and hugged her close. Although he wanted to, he didn't make an effort to kiss her. He just drew her close and held her.

Somehow, she realized, he knew she was terribly upset and was trying to comfort her.

"What happened?" he asked, standing Anna down on the floor and turning his attention to Evelyn.

"Anna, will you do Mommy a favor and go play for a few minutes? It won't take long, but I need to talk with Adam."

"But Mommy! I need to talk with Adam, too!" Total exasperation sounded in each word. "I always have to go play when you and Adam talk."

Adam squatted down to get on eye level with Anna and said, "Go play for a few minutes, then if Mommy wants to, I'll take you and her to see my house. And I may have a puppy you can play with, too!"

"Can we, Mommy? Can we go to his house and see the puppy?"

"If you'll go play until I call you, then I think maybe we can," Evelyn promised.

As Anna ran off to amuse herself, Evelyn looked at Adam. "A puppy? You really do play dirty, don't you?"

"Honestly, I got Mangy several weeks ago. He was the only one left of a litter that one of the church members had and couldn't afford to keep, so I took him."

"Mangy? Is that really a good name for a poor puppy?"

"Wait until you see him. I've never seen a dog as ugly as this one is. Nor have I ever seen one as sweet as he is. I'm in love with that ugly mutt, and I think you and Anna will feel the same.

"But what happened last night that changed your mind so quickly?"

"I saw a drug deal go down, right out there in the parking lot. And the guy who sold the drugs went back into apartment 12C. Adam, he's my neighbor. You were right, I can't let Anna live under these circumstances."

"Did you actually see the drugs?"

"No, but he handed the other guy a package and the other guy gave him some money. Don't you believe me? You're the one who warned me."

"I totally believe you, but I was trying to decide if we need to report it to the police or not. I don't think there's enough evidence they can use, so I'll just make a casual call in a few days and say that a member of the church saw this, but can't prove it. That will alert them to watch these apartments more carefully. Did you get a look at the seller's face?"

"No, he had on a ball cap and his face was in the shadows."

"Okay, then we don't really have anything to go on."

Now was not the time to have second thoughts, Evelyn reminded herself. But what was she about to do? She still couldn't believe her life had gotten to a point where she had to accept a practical stranger's proposal because she'd made the bad decision to marry Darren Carmichael.

"You're not getting cold feet, are you?" Adam said, taking her chin and tilting her head up to look at him.

"What if we just rented a couple of rooms from you?" Evelyn blurted out. Where had that come from? she wondered.

"Sure. That would go over really well. Can you imagine the talk that would stir up among the members? 'Can you believe Pastor Adam is living with a woman who has a child and they're not even married? Maybe the little girl is his and he just hasn't said anything.'"

Evelyn couldn't keep back the laugh that escaped her at Adam's portraying someone talking behind their hand and the silly look on his face.

"Yeah. Maybe I didn't think that one through very well. I forgot for a moment that you have an image to keep up," Evelyn said.

"So are you ready to go see your new digs?" Adam asked.

Chapter 6

AFTER GETTING ON HARDING PLACE, IT DIDN'T TAKE LONG for them to turn left on Franklin Road.

"These houses and lots are huge! And beautiful," Evelyn said, trying to take in everything as they drove by.

"There are a lot of old homes on this stretch of Franklin Road," Adam said. "I don't know if you know much about country music, but Ronnie Milsap lives on this road. Webb Pierce and George Jones and Tammy Wynette also had homes here.

"You can also get to Radnor Lake from Franklin Road. Radnor Lake is the largest pocket of wilderness in the U.S. close to a major city. The hiking trails and area have some awesome views."

Soon they turned off Franklin Road onto a side street, then into a long, curving driveway. Evelyn saw a huge white house perched on a knoll in the distance.

"There it is," Adam said.

"This is your house?" Evelyn asked in an astonished voice as she took in the two-story house they were approaching. Wrap-around porches for the first and second floors were decorated with hanging baskets and inviting seating areas.

"Just wait until we get closer, then you'll understand what I meant when I said I rattle around in the house. It has fifty-six-hundred square feet in it, five bedrooms—and each bedroom has its own full bath—along with a host of other very modern amenities.

"Mrs. Smith had it totally remodeled a few years ago to modernize it, because she planned to sell it. But when it came time, she just couldn't do it.

"Her grandfather had built the house for his wife and son, Mrs. Smith's father, after he became owner of one of the larger banks in town. He and his wife had wanted to fill the house up with children, but after the one son was born the wife couldn't have any more children.

"Then Mrs. Smith's parents only had her and she and her husband couldn't have children, so she had no family to leave the place to, but she wanted to hold on to it.

"At first I was completely uncomfortable with the idea of accepting the house, but her lawyer convinced me that this was what she wanted with all her heart, so I gave in."

They had been stopped in front of the house for a few minutes as Adam talked. "Are you ready to see the inside?" he asked.

"I am!" Anna piped up from her back seat car seat. "I want to see my puppy!"

"*Your* puppy?" Evelyn asked. "Who said it was your puppy?"

"I did," Anna answered, climbing out of the back seat when Adam opened the door and unfastened her car seat. "It will be mine because I can love it the most!" she declared.

"I think you're probably right," Adam said,

"Please don't encourage her brazen presumptions," Evelyn pleaded.

Adam took Anna's hand and put his arm around Evelyn's shoulder and guided them up the pristine white steps to the bottom porch.

Evelyn wanted desperately to glance around to see if anyone was watching, but decided the house was too far off the road for anyone to tell who was going inside.

As Adam unlocked the door and they entered a large foyer, he turned quickly and punched some numbers on a modern-looking security pad.

"This was part of the remodel," Adam explained when he saw Evelyn looking at him. "The first impression of the house is that it's an early 1900s house, and it is, but don't let that worry you. Mrs. Smith and her decorators did an excellent job in staying true to the time period of the house while installing all the modern fixtures anyone could want.

"For instance, that old church pew was the pew her grandparents sat in when they attended church. When the church was refurbished, she got the pew. But the recliner beside it is a La-Z-Boy. So there's that kind of beautifully mixed blend throughout the house."

Immediately to the left, off the foyer, was a curved grand staircase leading to the second floor. Evelyn could clearly imagine young women with long, flowing dresses coming down those stairs to greet their guests or suitors.

At that moment one of the ugliest dogs Evelyn had ever seen came racing from an adjoining room and ran straight to Anna and started jumping on her, wanting to play.

"See, Mommy, I knew he would love me!" Anna said, kneeling and wrapping her arms around the puppy.

Evelyn didn't think she'd ever seen an uglier dog. Blond and white hair intermingled all over the dog's body—if you could call it hair. Part spikes and part waves fought for domination of the poor little fella's body. The ears didn't stand up, nor did they flop. They hung straight out to the sides like airplane wings. Beautiful, soft brown button eyes and a smut-black nose and lips stood starkly out from the mingled blond and white spiky hair on his face.

The old saying about something being so ugly it was cute came to Evelyn's mind while she instantly fell in love with the expression on the pup's face.

"Well, I warned you," Adam said as he watched Evelyn's reaction.

"Oh, but look at that face!" she said. "That's a face that just shouts love and devotion."

"And I think he'll get as good as he gives," Adam said, looking at Anna, who was now sitting on the floor with Mangy sprawled across her lap.

"So you left him out to roam the house while you were gone?" Evelyn asked.

"No, Sally's in the kitchen making us some lunch, and she let him out when she heard us come in."

"Sally?" Evelyn asked, not being able to keep the surprise from her voice.

"Sally lives on the street we turned off of, not too far from here. She makes sure I have food to eat when I'm going to be home."

As if on cue, a tall, thin woman who looked to be in her mid-fifties came through the same door Mangy had come through. "Oh!" she said, and stopped. "I didn't expect you to be out here in the foyer. I'm sorry to interrupt." She stood and slowly took in Evelyn and Anna.

"Sally, this is Eve and Anna," Adam said, with no more explanation offered. "Eve, this is Sally Johnson. Anna, say hello to Mrs. Johnson."

"Hello, Mrs. Johnson," Anna said, barely glancing up from her newfound love.

"Hello, it's nice meeting you," Evelyn said with a smile.

But Sally Johnson didn't smile. She just turned to Adam and said, "I made chicken salad so you could have sandwiches. I also made some sweet tea, and you already have Coke in the fridge. I need to get home and fix lunch for Sam." And with that, she was gone.

"Hmm. That was awkward," Evelyn said.

And so it begins, Adam thought. In less than two hours half the church would know that Adam had a woman and a child in his house. Without a chaperone, even!

"Sally's the church pianist. She plays the piano and organ beautifully, but she's a quirky sort, for sure. You just have to try to ignore her odd personality."

Pending problems caused apprehension to curl in Evelyn's stomach. What was she letting herself in for?

"Let's take the tour, then we'll have some lunch," Adam said, trying not to think about the hullabaloo that would start as soon as Sally made it home to her phone. "Are we ready to take the tour?"

"Mangy and I will just sit here and wait for you to get back," Anna announced, still clutching the ugly little dog in her lap.

"Mangy can come with us," Adam said before Evelyn could respond. She felt a small flash of resentment, but didn't comment.

"We'll start with the bedrooms upstairs, first," Adam said, heading up the staircase. "All five of the bedrooms are decorated in a friendly, breezy style with just a touch of country décor here and there. Mrs. Smith said she wanted to leave a blank canvas for the next owner, but still wanted the rooms to be pretty while they waited for someone to claim them.

"Each bedroom has large floor-to-ceiling windows that look out over the grassy knoll the house sits on. And each window has a point of interest that's meant to be a mentally happy place for the viewer.

"She also gave two of the bedrooms slightly more décor than the other. For the daughter or son she never had, she decorated a room that would be easy to turn into a girl's or boy's room.

"Now, this is the master suite," he said, swinging open a heavy, beautifully carved wooden door.

Evelyn gasped at the size of the room. "My entire apartment would fit in here!" she exclaimed.

"Almost," Adam agreed. "This room alone has six hundred square feet, but that does include the bathroom."

Evelyn stood in awe and looked at the room. Very light blue paint covered the walls, and flowing, sheer white curtains with tiny pale-green leaves hung from the windows. In her mind's eye she could see the curtains blowing in the breeze on a warm day when the windows were open. The bed was huge, probably a king size, covered with what looked like a hand-stitched quilt. Instead of bedside tables, bookshelves full of books stood on each side of the bed. Across the room, in front of a huge fireplace, was a sitting area with a couch and chair, complete with reading lamps and a coffee table covered in magazines.

Slowly, Evelyn became aware that Adam was closely watching her. She couldn't make out the look in his eyes. For the first time since she'd met him, his eyes looked guarded. Was she imagining things, or was he trying to hide something? And suddenly a small trace of fear shot up her spine.

"Why are you looking at me like that?" she asked. She'd promised herself when she left Darren that never again would she let a man play head games with her.

A slow blush crept over Adam's face, but he recovered quickly and said, "If you think this is something, wait until you see the bathroom," and started walking in that direction.

"Adam," Evelyn said, reaching out and placing a hand on his arm to stop him. "I need to know why your eyes looked guarded just now. I can't get involved with another man who's going to play games with me, so we may as well work this out right now."

"Okay, if you insist," Adam said, moving a little closer to her and leaning near her ear so Anna couldn't hear him. "I suddenly got the vision of you sitting on the side of that bed in the morning, looking like you did yesterday. Just for the record, it shocked me, and I was trying not to let you see how that vision had affected me."

Now it was Evelyn's turn to blush. She was rewarded by Adam's soft chuckle, which sent sensuous chills up her spine.

"Okay, let's see the bathroom," Evelyn said, moving quickly away from Adam.

"Eve, I don't sleep in this room." His voice caused her to turn back to him. "I sleep in the one at the end of the hall. I like that view better, plus this room is just too big for me. I want you to have this room. And if things go right, one day I'll join you in it."

And now it was Evelyn's turn to have visions of being in this room with Adam. Sitting in front of a warm fire, reading or just talking. Waking up in the morning and looking out over the beautiful landscape. And lying beside him at night, after—

She realized her face had to be blood red by now, and by the huge grin on Adam's face, he knew just what was causing her red face.

"Well, well. I do believe I've just seen another side of the proper Ms. Carmichael." His eyes were green fire as he watched her.

"Can we puleeze see the bathroom now?" Anna's impatient voice interrupted the moment between the two adults.

"Right this way, ma'am," Adam said, taking Anna by the hand and leading them into a bathroom that Evelyn couldn't have imagined even after visiting some of Darren's very wealthy friends in Meridian. It had a Jacuzzi tub, a stand-alone shower, a closed-off toilet for privacy in case someone else was in the bathroom with you, and double lavatories in beautifully carved cabinets against an entire wall.

"Now, I'm thinking Mrs. Smith had the idea of a couple with children, or at least a child, owning this house, because there's a door here that leads to the next bedroom. Since the next bedroom has its own bath, there's no other reason for this door to go to that bedroom. And I think you'll see who'll want to claim it when you get the reaction," Adam said, giving Evelyn a knowing wink.

As soon as he opened the door to the adjoining room and let Anna go in, Evelyn heard a squeal of delight.

"Told you," Adam said, and stepped aside to let Evelyn go in the room.

"Mommy! Look at this! Can this be my room? Can Mangy stay in this room with me? Please, Mommy! Look, it's perfect for a little girl like me!"

"Sweetheart, slow down," Evelyn said, and stood looking around.

Adam lifted Anna and Mangy onto the bed and looked back at Evelyn. "See how perfect they look on that bed? In this room?"

"You really aren't playing fair, Adam Singletary," Evelyn declared.

The room was done in a light-pink paint with curtains that were a shade darker pink. The bed was covered with a pink comforter that was covered in nursery rhyme characters, and as she watched, Anna discovered the characters and became engrossed in trying to see just how many there were.

"Mommy, look! My favorites! All my favorites are on the bed!" Anna's eyes wouldn't have sparkled any more if it had been Christmas morning.

"I know, baby," Evelyn said. The bed had a white headboard and a matching chest of drawers set to one side. A small bookcase full of children's books stood on the other side of the bed. Across the room was a children's table with two small chairs snugged up under it. It was perfect.

In fact, it was *too* perfect.

"Adam, how much have you added to the décor of this room since we've been back from Meridian?" Evelyn asked, afraid of his answer, yet knowing that Mrs. Smith hadn't added the children's furniture, comforter, children's books, coloring books, crayons, and craft material that just happened to be the appropriate age for Anna.

"I haven't added anything to the room since you've been home from Meridian," he said, looking innocent.

Evelyn didn't miss his use of "home." "So Mrs. Smith wanted children so badly that she decorated this room for the four-year-old daughter she always wanted? Why didn't she decorate for a nursery first, instead?"

"Well, I didn't say that I didn't add a few things. I said I haven't added them since you've been home after going after Anna."

"Adam, can't you see how unfair this would be to Anna if I decided against moving in here? It would break her heart. She's already claimed this room as hers," Evelyn said, glancing over at Anna. She was astonished to see her little girl sound asleep with her arm around an ugly, sleeping puppy.

Tears sprang to her eyes at the sight, and she couldn't hide them before she looked back at Adam, who walked to her and took her in his arms. His arms felt wonderful holding her tightly against his chest, and for the first time in a long, long time Evelyn felt a sense of well-being settle over her.

CHAPTER 7

GIVING IN TO A DESIRE THAT HE'D FELT FROM THE FIRST time he saw her, Adam pulled away from Evelyn enough to catch her lips in a brief kiss that went straight to her heart. So light, so brief, yet so tender. But before she could react he said, "Let me help you. Let me be a part of your life. I really need that, and I think you and Anna need me, too."

Before she could answer he stepped away from her, but held on to one hand and pulled her toward the door. "Why don't we see the rest of the house up here, and after they get their nap we can go down and have lunch. We can hear them when they wake up."

Evelyn allowed herself to be drawn across the hall, where the next two bedrooms were.

"This one is my office. I spend a lot of time in here. I left the bed in here so I can just tumble into it at the end of the day when I have to work late. I don't do that very often, but sometimes. Also, if we have out-of-town guests that need to stay over, I can sleep in here and let them have all the other bedrooms if there are several people, or a big family."

Several bookshelves filled with books stood against the walls. A huge antique desk was almost covered up with a computer, printer, fax machine, scanner, and several other items that Evelyn didn't recognize. She could understand how a person could spend a lot of time here.

Occasionally, without being aware of doing it, she would touch her fingers to her lips because she could still feel the results of Adam's kiss. She knew, without thinking about it, that Darren had never, not even once, kissed her that tenderly.

"Eve?" Adam's voice finally penetrated her thoughts. "Are you okay? Am I boring you to tears?"

Evelyn quickly lowered her hand from her mouth and shook her head. "I'm sorry. I was remembering something that I shouldn't even be thinking about."

"Want to share it?"

"No!" she answered too quickly. "I mean, no, I'm okay. Really. Now tell me again what I missed."

"Well—" the twinkle that sparked in his eyes alerted Evelyn that mischief was on the way. "I'm not sure where I lost you."

"You were saying that you sleep in here sometimes when you work late, or if you need all the bedrooms for out-of-town guests."

Adam saw the last part sink in. Her beautiful amber eyes grew even larger than they normally were, and her perfectly kissable lips pursed in an "O" of understanding.

"Now, before you panic, let me assure you that out-of-town guests won't be your responsibility at all. There are several women in the church who jump in and take care of food, making the beds, cleaning the house, and anything else that may need to be done. They enjoy doing it, and will be disappointed if we don't let them keep doing what they do.

"Plus, with you and Anna here, taking up two of the bedrooms, I won't be able to invite as many folks in. But there are plenty of other church members who will be more than happy to fill in where we can't."

"Adam, that brings up another thought. This is a huge

house, and I'm not sure that I can keep it up, plus work at the store and take care of Anna when we move in here."

Realizing what she'd just said, Evelyn popped both hands over her mouth and looked at Adam with huge eyes as her face slowly started to burn. Why had she said that? She hadn't totally made up her mind yet!

The laugh that rolled out of Adam bounced off the walls. He took her hands and kissed both her palms before saying, "Don't say a word. Just listen. Sally does all my cooking, unless I specifically tell her I don't need for her to. I tried to get her to stop once, and I really think I highly insulted her. So I'm sure she'll love to continue cooking for us.

"Betty Lucas and Amy Moore come over once a week and clean the house whether it needs it or not. They declare that they love the house and pretend it's theirs while they clean it. And I'm sure they'll want to continue.

"The church pays all these ladies. Since the church doesn't have to provide a parsonage for me, they feel like they need to do something. So you won't have to worry about anything except your and Anna's laundry.

"Now that the horrified look has mostly left your face, come on and let me show you the other two rooms," he said, and led her from his office.

As they stepped into his bedroom, Evelyn was aware of being surrounded by Adam Singletary. The room was painted in pale yellow, with light tan curtains framing the windows. A deeper yellow chenille bedspread covered the queen-size bed. A large leather recliner sat in the corner by a small round table that had several books open on it, as if he'd been reading them all. Solid oak furniture completed the room.

She caught a slight hint of his cologne. One of his shirts was draped over the end of the bed, and a pair of house slippers waited to be slipped on when he was ready for them.

"Not much to say about this room. What you see is all pretty self-explanatory. These are my parents," he said, pointing to a photo that rested on his chest of drawers.

Evelyn moved closer to look at his parents. She could see his features in both of their faces. He'd obviously gotten his dad's height, but his mom's green eyes and open smile.

Why hadn't she ever wondered about his family? The fact that he had one had never crossed her mind. Was she so caught up in her own problems that she didn't open her thoughts to other people?

"You look like both of them," she said, glancing at him. "Where do they live? And why haven't you ever mentioned them?"

"They live in Memphis. I grew up there, but have moved around a lot. You know, following churches that thought they needed me."

"Do you have any siblings?"

"No, I'm an only child. I always wanted a lot of siblings and a big family, but my parents both have business careers and didn't want any more kids. Actually, I was an accident. They probably wouldn't have had any children if I hadn't surprised them."

"Do you ever see them?" Suddenly the thought of having to pretend to be married around his parents struck fear in her heart.

"We're kind of at odds. They never approved of my career choice, so words were said, feelings were hurt, and it's been around five years since I've seen them. I call about once a month, just to check on them, but I usually get Dad, and the conversations are brief and curt. I think Mom sees my caller ID on the phone and just hands the phone to him. When I ask to talk to her, Dad always makes some kind of excuse as to why she can't come to the phone. I'll keep trying to breach the gap, and hopefully one day we can be a family again."

"I'm so sorry I brought it up," Evelyn said, hearing the

sadness in his voice.

"No, you need to know that I have baggage hanging around my neck. I don't know of many human beings that don't have a certain amount of baggage here and there."

After a few more minutes in his bedroom Adam showed her the fifth bedroom, which was done in pale green as tastefully as all the others, with white curtains that had small yellow sunflowers on them and a yellow bedspread with faint blue swirl designs.

Finally they made their way down the hallway to where they left Anna and Mangy sleeping, and were surprised to see Anna sitting in one of the small chairs with a crayon and piece of paper, drawing a picture. Mangy was curled up at her feet, peacefully sleeping.

"Hi, Mommy! Hi, Adam!" Anna called when she saw them walk into the room.

"What are you doing?" Evelyn asked, walking to her and being aware that Adam had followed and stood closely beside her.

"I'm drawing my family," Anna said.

Evelyn saw a man, a woman, a little girl, and a dog, all drawn in a typical stick-figure childish rendition. Her first reaction was sadness that Anna was still hanging on to Darren. But she knew it would take Anna a while to let him go.

"See, this is Adam, you, me, and Mangy. We make a beautiful family, don't we?"

Shock weakened Evelyn's knees. This situation was rocketing out of control. She should never have agreed to come here today. Her baby was going to get hurt all over again. What kind of mother would she be if she brought Anna into this beautiful home and allowed her to learn to love the place and to love Adam, then have to snatch it all away from her again? She would just have to find another apartment and raise Anna on her own.

"Breathe, Eve. Just breathe," Adam said quietly. "Don't panic on me, now. Let's finish our tour and have some lunch, then we can talk more about our plans."

"Our plans? No, Adam! These are *your* plans that you've made without involving me a whole lot! I feel like I'm being ramrodded into something I've lost control of. I will *not* be put into that situation again. Do you hear me?" She ended by jabbing her finger in his chest repeatedly.

Adam had caught her hand to stop the painful jabs, but before he could say anything Anna spoke in a very quiet voice. "Mommy, you're shouting again and saying some really bad things to Adam. I don't like it. Adam is being very nice to us, and you need to say 'thank you' and stop being mean to him."

Defeated, Evelyn snatched her hand from Adam's and walked to the bed and sat down. "I give up! You two have ganged up on me, and I don't have anywhere to turn." Tears rolled down her cheeks as she glared at her child and the man who stood looking at her.

Suddenly Adam was kneeling in front of her. He wiped the tears from her cheeks and said, "Please don't cry, Eve. I can't stand to see that. I'm sorry. You're right, I've pushed at you too hard. I should have stopped and realized that you're coming out of an abusive marriage and my pushing at you would only turn you the other way."

Anna snuggled into her mom's side and handed her a tissue from a box that was on the bedside stand. "I'm sorry I made you cry, Mommy. I'm sorry."

Adam put his arm around Anna and said, "We both made you cry, and we're both sorry. We'll try not to do that again, okay?" His eyes pleaded with Evelyn to forgive him.

"Okay," she whispered, and placed her arms around both of them in a tight hug.

She was right. How could she fight those two faces before her? She'd just have to go with the flow and work the problems out as they came along. She really hoped there wouldn't be too many.

She needed a break from problems, but she was afraid they were only beginning.

CHAPTER 8

EVELYN SMILED AS SHE PULLED AWAY FROM THE TINY TOTS Child Care building. Anna had walked in and made friends immediately with two little girls who were around her age. She barely took time to say goodbye to Evelyn as she left.

Evelyn felt completely at ease with the day care staff. And thankfully, the day care was only a short distance from her shop, so if Anna needed her she could be there in just a few minutes.

All Anna had talked about last night was going to live with Adam in "her" new home. Evelyn had tried to gently remind her that they might not live in that house, but Anna had been convinced they would live there with Adam and Mangy, and had referred to Mangy as "her dog" on several occasions. Evelyn knew she had to make a decision quickly for more reasons than one. Early this morning she'd seen another incident in the parking lot that looked like a drug exchange.

She'd hoped to get to the boutique before Julie and have a few moments to check things out and go over any problems that may have developed while she was in Mississippi, although Julie had assured her everything had gone smoothly. She was so grateful to have Julie working for her.

But as soon as she reached the door she realized that Julie was already there, as well as several customers. Checking her watch, she confirmed that it was five minutes until time to open the store. So why had Julie let customers in so early?

"Welcome to The Woman's Boutique," Julie called as soon as she heard the chime that let her know someone had come through the door. Then, looking up, she saw Evelyn and said, "Hey, Eve! It's so good to see you back!"

As if on cue, all eyes in the store turned and looked at Evelyn. Instant awareness that something wasn't quite right filled Evelyn, but she forced a smile and said, "Good morning, everyone. Let me put my stuff up and I'll be with you in a moment."

As she passed Julie she whispered "What is going on?" and headed for the back office.

Julie followed her and quickly said, "I'll explain later. Just help me get these people waited on and out of here so we can talk."

Curious eyes again turned to Evelyn as she and Julie went back into the shop and Evelyn took control of the situation. She hadn't lived and endured the public lifestyle with Darren without being able to stand strong under deep scrutiny, and scrutiny was what she was experiencing this morning. Suddenly she remembered Sally Johnson at Adam's house, and knew the grapevine had probably been up and running for a couple of days.

With a smile that could melt butter Evelyn asked, "Does anyone need help finding something? Who was here first? Julie and I will be happy to help you."

"I'm just looking," several voices murmured in unison.

"I know, and it's not at merchandise," Julie whispered beside Evelyn.

"Be nice, Julie," Evelyn whispered back, with a smile to let Julie know she wasn't scolding her.

After about thirty minutes all of the "customers" had left the store. Most of them had actually bought something, which almost made it worth the ordeal to Evelyn.

Julie came from the office carrying two cups of coffee, and handed one to Evelyn. They looked at each other and broke into peals of laughter. "Talk about being in a fish tank!" Julie exclaimed.

"I know," Evelyn sighed deeply. She'd believed that leaving Darren and moving to this larger city would keep her forever from having to live in the public eye. But then along came Adam Singletary, pastor extraordinaire—and here we go again!

"And this was just the beginning," Julie said. "You've been bombarded with messages in the past couple of days. I've written them down with the return phone numbers, but I don't see how you can answer them all. What happened to cause this uproar?"

"Anna and I met Sally Johnson a couple of days ago when Adam was showing us his home. Sally was there making lunch, and Adam speculated that she'd be on the phone as soon as she got home, spreading the word about him having a woman and child at the house. Apparently he knew what he was talking about."

"Adam showed you and Anna his house? And Sally Johnson saw you there? Oh, Eve, what was he thinking? He *knew* what a stink that would stir up!

"And why was he showing you his house? He's never offered to show it to me, and I've hinted that I'd love to see it. What's going on, Eve? What are you not telling me?"

Before Evelyn could answer the door opened and several more women came into the shop.

This went on all day, with Evelyn and Julie barely having time to grab lunch between customers. Did these women not know how conspicuous they were? It was obvious that The Woman's Boutique was a store with larger sized clothes. Under the name of the store was printed "Sizes 12 and Up." But a lot of the women flowing into the store were much smaller than a size 12.

The only good thing about it was that most of them bought something just so they didn't look so conspicuous. They sold more jewelry that day than Evelyn could have imagined, just because jewelry was the only thing in the store that would fit some of them.

Finally, when it came time to close, Evelyn said, "Julie, can you stay for a little while? I'll go get Anna and we'll come back here so you and I can look at the messages that have come in. You can take the hours off of another day. Either come in late or go home early."

"That's perfect, Eve! I have so many questions to ask you, I'll be willing to stay as long as you want. Jim is going fishing tonight, so I'll be at home alone."

"So you want me to bring pizza and we can just eat while we talk?" Evelyn asked.

"Again, perfect! I'll straighten up while you get Anna."

Anna chatted happily about her day while Evelyn picked up the pizza and drove back to the boutique. *At least Anna had a great day,* Evelyn thought as she parked her car. She was so thankful for that.

It was getting close to dark. A few sprinkles of cold rain had started as they walked from the car to the door, which Julie unlocked and swung open just as they reached it.

"Come in and give Aunt Julie a hug," she said to Anna, and gathered the child close. Julie and Jim didn't have children yet, and Julie had fallen in love with Anna as soon as she met her. Anna had taken it upon herself to start calling her Aunt Julie.

After getting Anna settled with her pizza and a carton of milk that Evelyn had ordered from the pizza outlet, the two women sat down with their pizza. The first thing Julie said was, "Okay, talk to me! Why were you at Adam's house? Is something going on with you two? I know he's really attracted to you, but do you share the feelings?"

"I'm sorry, Julie, but I have to eat now. Then after I eat, I have to go over those messages. Then after we do that, I will plead the fifth!"

"Oh, no, you don't! As far as I can tell, I'm the closest thing you have to a friend in this town, and if you shut me out I'll turn on you like a ticked-off hound dog. I'll just sulk around and not even act like you're in the world!"

The two laughed together, and Evelyn felt a weight lift off her shoulders when she realized that Julie was, indeed, a good friend. How long had it been since she'd had a real friend? Her friends in school had all grown up and moved on with their lives, and Evelyn knew that none of the women she'd met during her marriage to Darren had been real friends. Just acquaintances. So why not treat Julie as a friend and confide in her? Maybe a little girl-talk would make her decisions easier.

"Well, you do drive a hard bargain, Julie," Evelyn said, and reached out and touched Julie's arm. "Okay, I'll talk. And I know that I don't have to say this, but, please let this just be between the two of us."

Then she told Julie about Adam's proposal. About the apartment where she lived and how dangerous she now believed it was. She told her about how Anna had fallen in love with Adam's house and the dog named Mangy.

"Wait," Julie interrupted her, as she had been doing on occasion to comment or ask a question. "He named his dog Mangy? That man is really different, isn't he?"

Again they laughed, and Evelyn continued. "Julie, I'm so scared! I don't want Anna to get into another situation where she'll be hurt if Adam and I realize this marriage of convenience just isn't going to work. I can't stand seeing her hurt again by another man. I want her growing up respecting men, not hating them because they always hurt her."

"Okay, the way I see things from where I'm sitting is that this marriage may start out as one of convenience, but I don't believe it will stay that way. I've watched how Adam looks at you, and I'm convinced the good pastor is already over halfway in love with you. And I see how you react when he's around. Your breathing gets faster and your cheeks get a little flushed, so methinks there's more to how you feel about him than you even realize—or that you're admitting to.

"So my wise advice to you is, take a chance, Eve. Don't pass up a good thing just because you've been burned once. And from what you've told me, if you don't marry Adam, that lamebrained Darren will surely try to take Anna from you. Can you take the chance that he might win?"

Tears welled up and spilled down Evelyn's cheeks. "Will you promise to hold my hand through this, Julie? I'm going to need help. I don't have any idea how to deal with disgruntled church members, and I'm sure there will be some. I don't have any idea how to be a pastor's wife. Yes, I'm a Christian, and I spent time in church when I was younger, but that's as much training as I have to take on this job, and that's not much!"

Julie grasped Evelyn's hand. "I've got you covered, girl. I'll never let go, and I'll be by your side anytime you need me. Adam is a good man, and he'll lead you through all the tough spots when it comes to all the churchy things. You're a good woman, and Adam needs a good woman by his side. The two of you will make this church stronger and a better place to be. And hopefully, the two of you will help the church become a less stale and bogged down place. I've gone to church there since I was a child, but, honestly, lately, in spite of all Adam is trying to do, I've been looking around for somewhere else to go."

"I hope you're right, Julie. But you've helped me make my decision. It looks like I have a marriage proposal to accept."

CHAPTER 9

As Evelyn and Julie were getting ready to leave the shop, Evelyn's cell phone rang. Glancing at the caller ID, she saw that it was Adam. "Hello?" she answered the phone.

"Eve, where are you and Anna?"

Did she hear panic in his voice? "We're still at the shop, Adam. Is something wrong?"

"Thank God!" he exclaimed into the phone. "Just stay there until I can get there. I'm on my way."

"But, Adam—" Evelyn tried to explain that they were getting ready to leave, but he'd already hung up.

"What's wrong?" Julie asked.

"I don't know. He said to stay here and that he was on his way here."

"That doesn't sound good," Julie said. "I wonder what's happened."

They had turned the night lights on in the store earlier, and only had the regular lights on in the office where they'd eaten and talked.

"Should we turn the lights on so he can see we're here?" Julie asked.

"No, I told him we were here. We'll just wait until he gets

here, then let him in. If we turn the overhead lights on, I'm afraid someone will think we have a problem."

It wasn't long before they saw car lights pull up out front. Evelyn went to the door and opened it when she saw Adam get out of the car.

As soon as he was in the door, he closed it and grabbed Evelyn in a tight hug, then dropped to his knees when Anna ran to greet him. He wrapped his arms around Anna and buried his face in her hair for a few moments while saying, "Thank you, Jesus, thank you!" When he lifted his face to Evelyn, she saw that it was wet with tears.

"Adam, you're scaring me! What happened?"

Reaching behind him to make sure the door was locked, he said, "Let's go to your office so nobody passing by can see us through the window."

After everyone got to the office, Adam said, "Did you see anything out of the ordinary happening at the apartments this morning?"

"I thought I saw another exchange go down," Evelyn answered. "Why?"

"Did anyone see you watching? Did you do anything that may have let them know you saw them?"

After thinking for a few moments, Evelyn answered, "I'd turned on my living room light when I went to the kitchen to make coffee. Then I heard a car motor in the parking lot, and after seeing the other exchange I decided to check it out. So I turned my living room light off and peeked out the curtain, but I don't think they saw me do that."

"Well, I think someone did. Evelyn, there was a drive-by shooting at the apartments about an hour ago. Several bullets went through the front wall and into the living room where you and Anna would have been, if you'd been home. One of the bullets went through Anna's toy box and embedded in the back of the couch where you usually sit. The cops don't know if it was a random shooting, a warning, or an attempt to hurt someone."

Evelyn dropped into a nearby chair as the strength left her legs. If they'd gone home at their usual time, she or Anna could be hurt or dead by now. "But how did you know?" she asked Adam.

"I was watching the news and eating my dinner when I saw your apartment complex surrounded by police cars. I heard the announcer say there'd been a shooting, so I didn't wait, I just jumped in my car and headed that way.

"The cops assured me that nobody was in the apartment, and then I realized that your car wasn't there, so I called you."

"You can't go back there," Julie spoke up. "You and Anna can stay with me until they get this cleared up."

"But I'll need to go and get some things for tomorrow," Evelyn said.

"No. The police have the area marked off as a crime scene, and they told me they wouldn't let anyone come or go until they had all the evidence they could gather. They won't let you in tonight, or possibly even tomorrow," Adam said. Evelyn noticed his hand shaking as he raked it through his hair.

"Okay, I can take clothes from the shop to wear tomorrow, but I'll have to run by Walmart and pick up something for Anna."

"Why don't we do this—we'll leave your car here, and you and Anna can ride with me and I'll follow Julie to her place. I'll see you inside, and then I'll go to Walmart and get Anna some things for tomorrow. You can write her sizes down and I'll pick them up and bring them back to you."

"Adam! Don't you think you're overreacting? We'll be fine!"

"Look, I know I'm spitting out orders, and yes, I may be overreacting, but baby, I saw the bullet holes in Anna's toy box and in the couch. I'm scared, okay? I don't know how much these people know about you. I don't know if they took your license plate number when you left this morning. I don't know if they're waiting around the corner to do you more harm. Just humor me. Please."

Evelyn gave in. "Okay, okay. We'll do whatever you want." She had the passing thought that Darren had never acted like he cared for her safety at all, much less this much. But in all fairness, she had been much safer in a gated community than she was in the low-rate apartment complex.

After Adam checked outside to make sure no lurkers were around, they headed for Julie's. It wasn't long until they were tucked in at her house, all doors and windows had been checked to make sure they were locked, and Adam had finally left to buy Anna a set of clothes for the next day.

ADAM STOOD in the children's section of Walmart, feeling very conspicuous since it was his first time to shop for a child. He looked at the piece of paper with Anna's sizes on it. *Of course it had to be the little girl's section,* he thought as he picked up a pair of white socks with pink lace around the top. He smiled at how small and cute they were, and had a sudden longing for a child of his own. *Hold it!* he cautioned the unexpected urge. *Not the time or place.*

He'd found an equally cute pair of ruffled panties and was looking at the dresses when he glanced up and his eyes clashed and locked with Sally Johnson's. *Of course!* he thought. *Of course.*

Then that mischievous nature that his mom always told him would be his downfall popped up.

"Hello, Sally," he said, as if nothing at all was out of the ordinary. "You met Eve and her little girl, Anna, the other day. Do you think this dress will fit Anna?" The dress was the size Evelyn had given him, but Sally Johnson didn't have to know he had sizes.

Looking shocked at finding Pastor Adam in the little girl's

section of Walmart but trying to hide her surprise, Sally walked closer and looked at the pretty pink dress with tiny kittens all over it.

"Well, I didn't get a real good look at the little girl because she was sitting in the floor, but the label says it should fit ages 4–5, and that's about her age, isn't it?"

"Yes, she's four," Adam answered. "So I think I'll just take this one. It should work with the socks and panties I have in the cart."

Sally Johnson glanced in the cart and saw the socks and panties with nothing else in the cart, and Adam saw her thin eyebrows go up just a notch.

"Is it her birthday?" Sally asked.

"No, there was a drive-by shooting at the apartment where they live, so they can't go back there tonight. In fact, I'm not sure when they can go back. But thanks for your help. I'll see you tomorrow when you come over to fix my lunch." And Adam headed for the checkout lane, leaving Sally Johnson starring after him with her mouth gaped open.

That was just mean of me, Adam thought a moment later. He looked around for Sally, thinking he should apologize, but when he located her she was already on her cell phone.

ADAM TOOK the clothes to Julie's house and was happy that Evelyn and Julie approved of what he'd picked out. Anna was already sound asleep and it was late, so he made arrangements to pick them up the next morning. Then, reluctantly, he went home.

AFTER DROPPING Anna off at day care the next morning, Adam pulled into a parking space and told Evelyn, "I'm not happy about you being in the store today. If these people know where you work, they might come to the store and try to hurt you. Why don't you just hang out with me today?"

"Adam, you'll never know how much your caring attitude means to me. I don't even know how to react to it. Darren didn't act like this, even on our honeymoon. I want you to know that it touches me, and I appreciate it, but I'm not going to hide from a threat that may or may not exist."

"But what about Anna, if they did hurt you? Or kill you? Where would that leave her?" Adam could tell by the color leaving her face that he'd finally made his point. He didn't want to be cruel, but he didn't think Evelyn understood the magnitude of the situation she was in.

After staring into space for a few seconds, he said, "Let's get married tomorrow."

At Evelyn's quickly indrawn breath, he raised his hand and laid it on her shoulder. "Just hear me out, please, Eve. There's no blood test or waiting period after getting a marriage license in Tennessee. We could get the license today, and get married tomorrow. Then I could make arrangements to have your things moved into my house as soon as the police clear entrance into your apartment. You won't even have to go back there. I'm sure it's okay with Julie if you spend tonight at her house.

"We've talked about this. Anna loves the house, and I think you could learn to love it. And I promise you, I won't make any attempt to conjugate our marriage until you decide you're ready.

"But I will tell you this. I love you and want to spend the rest of my life with you. I knew when you walked into the church that first day that you were the woman I'd been waiting for. I don't know how I knew, but I knew. And Anna has my heart. I'll never intentionally do anything to hurt either one of you."

"But Adam, you're a minister. I don't know how to be a minister's wife. I don't know what I'm supposed to do. And you haven't even asked me if I'm a Christian or not. Isn't that supposed to play a role in a minister's marriage?"

"Christians don't come with papers of certification, Eve. A

lot of folks claim to be Christians but you can't tell it by the way they act. Then there are folks who've never been inside a church building but have all the characteristics of a Christian. Only God can tell what's in a person's heart.

"We can work through all of your fears as they come up. But right now, today, I feel like we need to protect you and Anna, and I'm convinced that hiding you under my name and my roof is the best way to do it. This will stop any of Darren's attempts to invalidate you as a fit mother, and it will discourage anyone who's trying to frighten you because of what you may have seen."

Evelyn stared into Adam's serious green eyes and felt her heart rate speed up. What was she about to do? Was she about to make the biggest mistake of her life?

Well, no, she reminded herself, marrying Darren had taken care of that feat, but still, this could rate right up there at the top if things didn't work out. But what choice did she have? She knew she had other choices, but she needed something to happen right now, and marrying Adam Singletary seemed to be the only quick solution.

Taking a deep, shaky breath, Evelyn said, "Okay, Adam. Yes, I'll marry you. God help me if I'm making a mistake, but my answer is yes."

Sliding closer to her, Adam pulled her close and held her. He didn't make any attempt to kiss her, although that was uppermost in his mind. "God help us both as we make this work out."

It sounded a lot like a prayer to Evelyn.

CHAPTER 10

THREE DAYS LATER FOUND EVELYN AND ANNA IN ADAM'S car, headed toward Meridian, Mississippi.

The day after the drive-by shooting at Evelyn's apartment Adam and Evelyn had gotten their marriage license, and the following morning Adam made arrangements for one of his minister friends to marry them in a quiet ceremony, with Julie and Jim standing with them to witness the marriage.

When it came time to exchange rings during the ceremony, Evelyn was surprised when Jim stepped forward and handed Adam two wide gold bands. Adam placed one on Evelyn's finger, and it fit perfectly. Then he handed her the one she was to put on his finger.

Exchanging the rings was an emotional shock for Evelyn. She wasn't expecting the sense of authenticity she felt when she looked into Adam's eyes as they slid the rings on each other's fingers. It was as if this was the real thing, and when she repeated the wedding vows the feeling of guilt she was expecting didn't show up. Just for a moment she could see herself spending the rest of her life with Adam Singletary.

Anna had been ecstatic that "they" were marrying Adam and Mangy and could go live in the "big" house. It was almost impossible to keep her still during the ceremony.

Just after the ceremony was over, Detective Greer from the Metro Nashville Police Department called Adam's cell phone and told him they could get into the apartment. They went over and picked up enough clothes for the trip, and then Evelyn and Anna went back to spend one more night with Julie and Jim, because the church didn't know about their marriage yet.

Adam had taken two weeks' vacation and left the flock in the care of the interim minister. He'd made arrangements with the church secretary to send a letter to all the congregation members announcing that he and Evelyn had gotten married and were on their honeymoon. In the letter he apologized for the suddenness of the wedding, and said he'd explain when they got back.

He knew he was setting them up for all kinds of speculation, but he and Evelyn had decided it was best to do it this way, so maybe the shock would have worn off a little by the time they got back and faced the congregation.

Plus, this would give him a chance to meet Evelyn's mom, and they could spend Thanksgiving with her while they were on their "honeymoon."

Evelyn had given Julie the go-ahead to hire someone to help her run the store while Evelyn was away. She trusted Julie, and didn't have to worry that everything would be fine. Julie could always call her if she ran into a problem.

"You sure are quiet," Adam said, glancing over at Evelyn.

Anna was contented in the back of the car in her car seat, with Mangy lying on the seat beside her. Evelyn figured they'd both be asleep before long.

"I think I'm just sitting here waiting for the past four days to sink in. But I'm having a hard time sorting it all out in my head."

"I know. It's been a whirlwind, but we have two weeks to try and figure out how we're going to work through the next few months," he said with a smile. "But I like a good challenge, don't you?"

"Adam, I'm just coming out of a really good 'challenge' and was hoping my life would become very calm and boring. But that's not going to happen yet, is it?"

"'Fraid not," he said, and patted her hand, which lay in her lap. "But together we can make this happen. It's going to be wonderful after the whirlwind settles down.

"Look in the back seat," he said, after glancing in the rearview mirror.

Looking around, Evelyn saw that the child and dog were sound asleep. Mangy had his head in Anna's lap, and her hand rested on top of the dog's head.

"The two of you are safe, and that makes it all worthwhile for me. I hope you believe me when I say that." He gently touched her cheek with the back of his fingers, causing an entire family of butterflies to jumpstart in her stomach.

Something had changed for her since the marriage ceremony. She couldn't be close to him without feeling an intensified reaction. Even now, sitting across the car from him, she imagined she could feel the heat from his body.

And he had become more attentive, if that was possible. Gently touching her like he'd just done. Or placing his hand on her shoulder when he was talking to her. Was he claiming her? Marking his territory by touching her? That thought brought an unexpected chuckle from her, and she quickly put her hand over her mouth and pretended to be coughing.

"Good try, Eve. Do you doubt what I said?"

Trying to hide her consternation, and searching her mind to try to remember what he'd said, she came up blank. She could feel her face turning red as she confessed, "I'm sorry, Adam, but what did you say?"

He laughed so loud that Mangy "woofed" in the back seat, then went back to sleep.

"How far back do I need to go?" he asked.

"I think you said something about us being safe."

"I said that makes all we've been through the past few days worth it to me."

Evelyn glanced into the back seat again and nodded. "I agree. Knowing that my baby is safe and happy makes it all worth it to me, too. I'd walk through hell and back for her. And Adam?"

"Yes, Eve?"

"I've been so wrapped up in my own problems, I haven't taken the time to think about all the sacrifices you're making for Anna and me. I don't understand why you're doing this, but I want you to know how much I appreciate it. I think you must be a man in a million to do what you've done. From the bottom of my heart, I thank you!"

It took Adam a moment to fight past the lump in his throat, and when he did speak, his voice was a little gruff. "This isn't all unselfishness on my part. As I told you, I recognized you as my woman the first day I saw you. Also, as I told you, having a wife will keep the matchmakers off my back. So don't make me out as too much of a goodie-two-shoes."

His woman? Evelyn had mixed emotions over that statement. Part of it made her feel secure, but the other part of her that never intended to be manipulated again rose to the surface. Was Adam going to be one of those husbands that became controlling and overbearing after the wedding dust had settled? She hadn't even considered such a thing.

"'Your woman?' I'm not sure how to take that, Adam. We had a neighbor who was a minister and who informed his wife, on a regular basis, that 'he was the head of the house and she was his helpmate and she was to do whatever he said to do.' That poor woman spent her life as his slave. You need to know up front that I'm not that type of woman."

"Do you know that the term 'help*mate*' isn't even in the

74

Bible? The term that that came from is 'help*meet*.' And the Hebrew word it's translated from is *ezer,* which is taken from the root word *azar,* meaning 'to rescue, succor, save and help.' It's used when talking about helping others or God helping us. It's a very strong word, but it's been diminished and misused by wrong-minded men who want to keep women 'in their place.' I can assure you that I'm not that kind of man, and I will never preach that kind of sermon. If I do, just shoot me when I get home!"

Evelyn was struck at the passion in Adam's voice as he spoke. But she was really relieved at his words. "Wow! That's amazing! I've always heard that a woman is a man's helpmate, and now I learn that it's a wrong use of a word."

"Throughout history the term 'helpmeet' has become 'help-mate,' but the original use in the King James Version of the Bible is 'helpmeet,' and both words mean 'help.' It's almost like saying a woman is a man's 'help help.'

"I'm really kind of fanatical about this, because I've counseled so many women who were going through hell at home, just like the neighbor you were talking about. A lot of men use this very term to rule over their wives like slave drivers instead of being loving, caring husbands."

Before Evelyn could comment, Anna spoke from the back seat. "Mommy, I have to use it!"

"Okay, baby. I'll bet Mangy has to use it, too," Evelyn answered.

"I just saw a sign for a rest area about a mile up the road. I'll pull in there," Adam said.

Evelyn was amazed at how patient Adam was about stopping as soon as someone sent the bathroom request. As soon as he found a roadside rest area or a ramp with a gas station or fast food restaurant, he pulled over. She remembered how much Darren hated to have to stop for anything other than food on the few trips they took. He just wanted to get there and have it over with.

Adam put the leash on Mangy and took him on a walk while Evelyn took Anna to the restroom.

They were just a little past Birmingham, which was around a hundred and eighty miles south of Nashville, but Evelyn could tell the temperature was already warmer than it had been in Nashville. Most of the trees here still had leaves on them, while the leaves around Nashville were almost all on the ground, even though it was still about a week and a half before Thanksgiving.

She was happy this had worked out so she could have Thanksgiving with her mom. Other than Christmas, Thanksgiving was her favorite holiday. She loved being with family, and had been dreading not being with her mom for the holiday.

After everyone was settled back in the car and they were on the road, Adam said, "Are you sure you don't want to tell your mom how our situation really is? I don't mind her knowing that ours is a marriage in name only for a while."

He never mentioned their marriage without throwing in that 'for a little while' stipulation, which always made Evelyn a little nervous. Would he just decide one day that he was ready to claim his marital dues? But he had promised to wait until she was ready, she reminded herself again, like she'd reminded herself all the times before.

"No. Like I said, I don't want her to have to lie to Darren if he should come nosing around asking her questions. And I don't put it past him to do just that. I'd just rather let Mom believe we're married for real."

"Well, you know that means we're going to have to act more like a happily newlywed couple in front of her. You can't act like you're afraid I'm going to touch you when I get close to you."

"I do not act like I'm afraid of you!" Evelyn denied. "Plus, Mom is kind of old-fashioned when it comes to showing public affection, so I'm sure we'll be okay just the way we are.

"But there's something I need to tell you. Mom has a boyfriend now, so I'm sure he'll be hanging around some. He's been helping take care of Mom while her shoulder heals."

"No problem. I'm glad she has someone to keep her company. But are you sure she won't expect me to keep my arm around you, or hold your hand and kiss you occasionally?"

Evelyn heard the teasing note in his voice, but her heart still took a leap in her chest at the thought of him being that attentive. "Yes, I'm sure she won't expect that," Evelyn assured him.

"Well, we'll see," Adam said.

"Adam Singletary, I forbid you to embarrass me in front of my mother! If you do anything that makes me uncomfortable, you know my face will get all red and she'll know something is up!"

"Oh, Eve, give your mom a break. She'll just think you're getting all turned on and excited."

"Adam! You—you're—"

But before she could get her thoughts out he burst into a loud laugh at her consternation.

"Okay, I promise to be good and not embarrass you, but, really, I'll need to occasionally do something to let your mom know that I love you. But I'll try to be discreet, okay?"

"Like what?" Evelyn asked, an uneasy feeling creeping over her.

"Oh, you'll know it when I do something. Trust me. Just play along, as if it's normal behavior."

"Adam, I'm not liking the sound of this."

"Oh, but I am," he said, with a chuckle that sent a warm wave over her body.

"Mommy, we're hungry," Anna called from the back seat.

And so it went until they reached La Quinta Inn in Meridian and parked.

Speaking quietly, so Anna couldn't hear him, Adam said, "It'll only take me a moment to run in and confirm our rooms, then we'll go to your mom's. I'd rather have this all done so after we visit we can just come back here and not worry about it."

"Are we there yet?" Anna called from the back seat.

"No, we're getting our room at the motel, then we'll go see Gramma."

"I'll be so happy to see Gramma! I've missed her so much. She makes really good cookies."

"Is that the only reason you've missed her?" Evelyn asked.

"No, I miss her for a lot of reasons, but I missed you more. I like living with Gramma, but I want to live with you. You're not going to leave me with her again, are you?"

"Oh, no, my darling. We're going to visit, and then we'll go back to Nashville."

"Back to Adam's big house? Please, Mommy. I love living there with Mangy."

"Anna, you haven't lived there yet!" Evelyn reminded her.

"In my mind I have," Anna said. "In my mind me and Mangy have run and played in the yard and had a really good time!"

"'Mangy and I have run in the yard,'" Evelyn corrected.

"Not in my mind, Mommy. It was just Mangy and me."

Evelyn was laughing when Adam sat back down in the car. "Are you two having a party without me?" he asked.

"No, just an English lesson that didn't take," Evelyn said.

He handed her two motel keys and kept two. "One is for my room and the other one is for your room," he explained.

"But why do we need each other's?" Evelyn asked.

"Just in case one of us forgets and leaves ours in the room," he answered. "Don't worry, I'm not going to sneak into your room at night. Although come to think about it, it will sure be tempting."

"Adam! Behave yourself! You aren't thinking like a minister," Evelyn admonished.

"Wanna bet? Eve, you have to remember that ministers are just human beings, just like everyone else. We have the same thoughts, desires, needs and temptations, just like anyone else. You've got to remember not to set ministers on a pedestal. The taller the pedestal, the farther we have to fall."

And with the thoughts he'd been having about this beautiful woman he was now married to, he'd have to climb up to even get on a pedestal, Adam thought.

CHAPTER 11

FOLLOWING EVELYN'S DIRECTIONS, IT DIDN'T TAKE LONG FOR them to reach her mom's house. It sat on a two-acre lot just south of Meridian, but still in the city limits.

"Nice," Adam said as he pulled to the front of the house and stopped. It was a typical ranch, probably built in the '50s, but the upkeep was immaculate. Huge oak trees surrounded it. "Did you grow up here?" he asked Evelyn.

"Yes. My parents bought this house when I was two years old, and I lived here until I left for college."

"Gramma!" Anna squealed as a small woman with pepper-gray hair started down the steps toward the car.

Evelyn got out of the car and helped Anna out while Adam put the leash on Mangy.

After Evelyn and Anna had gotten big hugs from her mom, Evelyn turned to Adam and said, "Mom, this is Adam Singletary. Adam, this is my mother, Sara Annabel Tew."

"Hello, Mrs. Tew," Adam said, offering her his hand.

"Oh, come here, son, and give me a hug! And you just drop the 'Mrs. Tew' thing and call me Sara," she said, wrapping Adam up in a warm hug.

"And this must be Mangy," Sara continued, reaching down

and patting Mangy on top of his head. "You're right, Eve, he really is an ugly dog."

At that point Mangy sat and raised a paw to her and whined. "Oh, just look at that. He may be ugly, but what a sweetheart!

"Y'all come on in and we'll get you something to drink. Adam, do you want some sweet tea, or would you rather have a soft drink?"

"Tea would be wonderful," Adam answered. He put his arm around Sara's shoulders and walked with her back up the steps to the front porch, leaving Evelyn and Anna to follow with Mangy.

The house had a total 1950s feel, with shining hardwood floors and furniture that was worn, but still in good shape. Evelyn glanced around the living room and was inundated with warm memories from her childhood. She breathed in the fresh scent of furniture polish and knew that her mom, in spite of still recuperating from the shoulder surgery, had been "spiffing up" the place before they got there.

Evelyn went directly to the mantel to look at the photo of her mom and dad on their wedding day. Both of them looked so happy. Sadness engulfed her for a moment, as the loss of her father hit her like it did every time she thought of him. And also knowing that she would probably never know the newlywed glow of happiness like the couple in front of her. She just didn't seem to be destined to have a happy marriage.

Evelyn reached up to wipe tears from her eyes, just as her mom put her arm around her waist and said, "Honey, it's been ten years since his accident. I know you still miss him. You were his princess. I miss him, too, but life must go on. Now come on in the kitchen and join us for some tea. That husband of yours is a real hunk!"

"Mom!" Evelyn said, surprised at her saying such a thing, and a little confused at her statement about life going on. Neither of those things sounded like her mom.

But her mother just chuckled and headed for the kitchen, where Evelyn found Adam and Anna sitting at the large table eating fresh-baked cookies and drinking her mom's wonderful sweet tea. It was good to be home.

Evelyn spotted a new dog bed lying by the kitchen door. "Mom, do you have a new dog?" she asked.

"No, that's for Mangy. I knew he'd need a soft spot to sleep, so I got it for him."

"Well, that was sweet," Evelyn said.

"Really, Sara, you didn't need to go to that trouble," Adam said. "In fact, if you don't want him to run loose in the house we can put him in the crate. We'll have to leave him in the crate when we leave the motel room, anyway."

"Nonsense!" Sara said. "I love for him to be in the house. I can tell Anna really loves him. And there won't be any leaving him in the motel room, because I want Mangy and Anna to stay with me while y'all are here. That will give the two of you some time alone. I mean, who ever heard of taking a child with you on a honeymoon? When me and my George went on our honeymoon—well, since there are young ears listening, I won't finish, but there's just not room for a child in the middle of a honeymoon."

When she finally took a breath, Evelyn said, "But Mom—"

"Now, you just hush, child! I've really missed Anna, and I need her here to help me bake cookies and pies and things for Thanksgiving. And we'll probably even take a day trip to the Jackson zoo, if we have time. Would you like to go to the zoo with Gramma and Fred?" she asked Anna.

"Mommy, can I? Can Mangy and I stay with Gramma and cook and go to the zoo? Please, please, puleeze!"

"See, it's a done deal," Sara said with a smile, and took more cookies from the oven.

"She's always been this way," Evelyn said to Adam. "My dad called her his tiny steamroller, because she could out-talk, out-think and outwit him before he could take a breath.

"Mom, is Fred coming over tonight?" Evelyn asked, wondering how much he actually came to visit. How close were they? Was her mom serious about this guy? Was that what she meant when she said "life must go on?"

But before Sara could answer Evelyn they were interrupted by the front door opening and a strong male voice calling, "Can I come in, or is this a private party?"

"Oh, get yourself in here and stop being dramatic!" Sara called.

Suddenly the room seemed to shrink as a very tall, very large man came into the dining room, walked straight to Sara and planted a smacking kiss on her cheek.

Evelyn instantly saw the change on her mom's face. Sara's green eyes, which had always held a sparkle, ignited with happiness.

"Adam, this is Fred Kelly. Fred, you met Evelyn during the time of my surgery, and you met Annabel when she was staying with me for a while. And this is Adam Singletary, who is now my son-in-law. My life feels totally complete today."

Evelyn had to fight the sinking feeling that came out of nowhere and centered in the pit of her stomach. She knew without being told that this man, this Fred Kelly, was going to take her father's place. She could see the love for him in her mom's eyes. She'd wondered about some of the looks her mom and Fred had shared when she was here for the surgery, but those looks were more obvious now.

She was torn between wanting her mom to be happy and not alone, but wanting to preserve the memory of her parents together, like she'd always known them. This was going to take some getting used to. But she'd think about it later. Today she wasn't going to cause problems for her mom.

Fred shook hands with Adam, then picked Anna up and held her over his head before wrapping her up in a bear hug while she giggled the entire time. "I think you've grown, Puddin'," he said, standing her on the floor. Then he turned to Evelyn and took both her hands in his.

"Eve, you're even more beautiful than I remembered. I see the doubt in your eyes, and I want to clear the air right now. I know it'll be hard to see your mom and me together to start with. Your mom has told me how much you still miss your dad, and how close the two of you were. I'm not here to try and take his place. He will always be your father, and I have no interest in being your father. I have three adult brats of my own, and I really don't want another one."

Evelyn suddenly understood why her mom loved this man.

"I just have one question," Evelyn said. "When are you two planning on getting married?"

"Talk about getting it all out in the open!" her mom exclaimed. Turning to Fred, she said, "Well, you jumped right in there and opened up this box of worms—shall we go ahead and tell her?"

Fred pulled Sara to his side and engulfed her with one arm. Evelyn realized that her mom's head barely came to Fred's chest pocket. Her mom could easily stand under his arm if he lifted it.

"We've been married for a month," Sara said. "We got married just before I had my surgery. Fred's been a wonderful nurse."

"But Mom, you two are still on your own honeymoon! You don't need to keep Anna and Mangy."

"Oh, no, honey. We had our honeymoon before we ever got married," Sara said, then clamped her hands over her mouth and looked at Adam, who roared with laughter.

"It's okay, Sara. I'm a minister, not a judge," Adam assured the embarrassed woman.

Fred leaned over and gave Sara a gentle kiss, then said, "Her honesty is one of the many things I love about Sara."

Adam, who had stood to get more tea, leaned close to Evelyn's ear and said, "Now, what was that about your mom being kind of old-fashioned?"

Evelyn elbowed him in the stomach and said, "Go away."

THE AFTERNOON passed quickly as preparation for dinner began. Fred put steaks on the grill, and he and Adam chatted and kept an eye on Anna as she played outside with Mangy.

In the kitchen Evelyn and Sara made a green salad, baked potatoes, and broccoli and cheese and chatted about how much Anna had grown in the short time she'd been gone.

Finally, Evelyn was tired of skirting around the issue and said, "Mom, talk to me about you and Fred. How did you meet? How long have you known each other? You know, just tell me about it."

"Okay, I will if you will. Eve, I didn't expect you to remarry for a long time after what you went through with that piece of scum Darren Carmichael. And now here you are married to a minister. So soon? Are you pregnant? I mean, I know he's a fine-looking man, but I'm just stunned at your actions."

Evelyn laughed and hugged her mom while she fought the overpowering surge of guilt at hiding the truth from her. "No, Mom, I'm not pregnant. And you're right, Adam is a fine-looking man. You know, you just never can tell when love will strike." Hoping that would satisfy her mom, she started getting plates and utensils out for dinner.

"Now you hold it right there," Sara said, coming to stand close to Evelyn. "I know my daughter. I know you don't just fall in love with someone just because he has a pretty face. And you haven't known him long enough for true love to set in."

"Don't you believe in love at first sight, Mom?" Evelyn interrupted. "You know it can happen. Obviously you didn't know Fred that long."

"I've known Fred a very long time," Sara said, with a brief

sadness passing over her face before she quickly hid it. "Fred is my best-kept secret. What I'm about to tell you is going to hurt you a little, but it takes nothing away from your father. Fred and I were sweethearts in high school. We were talking about getting married, but Uncle Sam called and Fred went into the Marines. We promised that we'd keep writing to each other and stay in touch, and when he got home we'd continue our courtship.

"But you know how long-distance courtship goes sometimes. He was stationed in California and met a young woman who swept him off his feet. She was there and I was here. Pretty soon his letters slowed down, then finally I got my 'Dear Jane' letter saying he was going to stay out there and make a life with Judy, his new love.

"I was heartbroken. It took me a year to finally get over him enough to move on with my life. I went dancing with a couple of girlfriends one Saturday night, and that night I met your father.

"It wasn't love at first sight, but we developed a friendship that eventually led to love. I loved your father with most of my heart. But there was always a small place in my heart that was still full of Fred. Maybe it was because I never got to say goodbye to him in person.

"About a year ago I got a phone call, and it was Fred. Judy had been dead for three years, and Fred was back in Meridian to take care of his aging mother. He'd learned that George was gone, and he wanted to know if we could meet for lunch one day.

"He was afraid I'd never forgive him for what he'd done, but said he could never totally forget me and could we just hang out sometimes. It didn't take too much hanging out for the old spark to reignite, and here we are.

"I hope you won't hold it against me for loving two men at the same time."

It took Evelyn several moments to process all that her mother had told her, but she realized that her parents had had a good, long life together, and her mom was too young to spend the rest of her life alone. Evelyn was suddenly overwhelmingly happy that her mom had Fred to spend the coming years with.

"I think I do understand, Mom. But even if I didn't, I'm not one of those adult children who want their parent to be alone and miserable just because I don't want to see you with someone else. It's kind of weird to see Fred being so affectionate with you. You and Dad never showed open affection when I was around."

"Your dad wasn't an openly affectionate man. He loved me, and I never doubted that, but he just didn't show it much. But now, Fred—Fred is extremely affectionate. I'll ask him to cool it if it makes you uncomfortable."

"Absolutely not, Mom. Just leave Fred alone and let him love on you whenever he wants to."

"Okay, I've confessed. How about you?"

"I told you everything there is to tell you," Evelyn said, sending up a prayer for forgiveness for lying to her mother.

"Nope. Not even close. Don't try to scam your mom. You were never able to do that."

"So you and Fred were becoming an item even while I was still living here with Darren?"

"Yes. We kept it hidden from you because I knew your marriage was in trouble and I didn't want you to know how happy I was while your world was falling apart. Now, child, stop trying to change the subject and tell me about you and Adam."

"Mom, the guys are heading in with the steaks! We'd better finish what we're doing so we can eat."

"Okay, but this isn't even close to the end of this conversation," Sara said, shaking her wooden stirring spoon at Evelyn.

CHAPTER 12

TWO HOURS LATER DINNER HAD BEEN FINISHED, THE kitchen cleaned, and Adam and Evelyn were getting ready to head back to the motel.

Evelyn peeked into the room where Anna had been tucked into bed. Mangy lay on top of the cover beside her. Both were sound asleep, tired from a long day.

Sara came to stand beside Evelyn and looked down on the two. "They're just precious together. I'm happy they'll be staying with me. I know it's going to be a long time between visits now, so I won't get to see her as much as I used to. I'll miss that."

Evelyn heard the sadness in her mom's voice, and turned to face her. "Mom, you and Fred can come to Nashville anytime you want to, and can stay as long as you want. Adam's house is huge. There's enough room for you and another family. And there's so much to see and do in Nashville. You'll love it there. So plan on coming soon."

"Now that's what I'm worried about. You didn't say 'our' house is huge, you said 'Adam's' house is huge. And Fred and I act more like newlyweds than the two of you. Tell me what's going on!"

Adam walked up just in time to save Evelyn from having to answer her mom. "Sorry to interrupt you two, but Fred wants to take me fishing tomorrow. Is that okay, or do you want to do something else?" he asked Evelyn.

"That's a fantastic idea," Sara said. "That will give me a chance to catch up with my daughter, then you two are going to have to take some time alone. This is, after all, your honeymoon."

"Eve?" Adam asked.

"Sure, that will be fun! Like Mom said, it'll give us a chance to catch up."

After Adam went back to the living room to tell Fred the fishing trip was on, Sara said, "This! This is what I'm talking about. A man doesn't go on a fishing trip with another man on the first day of his honeymoon!"

"Mom, we have to go now. We'll talk tomorrow. Okay?" Evelyn leaned over and kissed her mother on the cheek.

After saying goodnight to Fred, Adam and Evelyn headed for the car.

After riding for a few minutes, Evelyn said, "Mom's on to us. She's demanding answers from me. She said she and Fred act more like newlyweds than we do." She told him everything her mom had said while they were in the kitchen.

"What do you want to do? Do you want to tell her?" Adam asked.

"Not really, but I'm already in danger of hellfire because I've lied to my mother so much! So I guess we're going to have to come clean with her. She and Fred will probably sit up half the night trying to figure us out."

"Well, the fishing trip is a good idea, then. It will give you time to tell your mom about Darren threatening to try and prove that you were an unfit mother, about the apartment and how you weren't safe, and how I came about having the huge house and needed someone to help fill it up. And you can tell

89

her that I'm madly in love with you and am just waiting for you to catch up and realize you're in love with me."

By now they were at the motel, and Adam pulled into a parking space in front of their rooms and stopped the car. He was about to open his door when Evelyn reached out and stopped him by placing her hand on his forearm. It was the first time she'd ever casually touched him, and she was instantly aware of the strength she felt, even through the light jacket he had on.

He looked down at her hand resting on his arm, then back up into her eyes, and suddenly she couldn't remember what she was going to say to him. She became acutely aware that they were totally alone, at a motel, in a city where no church members could raise questioning eyes. Anna was safely tucked in at her mom's house. They were married.

She felt desire for her husband rush into her being as if Niagara Falls had taken a detour through her.

She knew her thoughts were causing her face to turn all different shades of red, and was sure he could see her pulse throbbing in her neck, even in the dim parking lot lights.

She snatched her hand from his arm as if she'd been burned. In fact, that's exactly what her hand felt like.

As if reading her mind, Adam placed his arm on the seat behind her and said, "Eve, I want nothing more than to go into one of these rooms with you and make love with you all night long. I want to lie between your breasts like that pendant that has hung there all day and taunted me, making me jealous that I can't be there. But I want you to be sure. I can't believe I'm saying this, but make certain this is what you want before you commit. Because once we cross that bridge, I'm not sure I can ever go back. I meant what I said about being madly in love with you. This trip down here and seeing you with your mom has just added flames to my fire. I'm fascinated with everything about you.

"Now, I think we should go inside and try to get some rest. We can take this up at another time when you're not so tired, physically and emotionally."

Still stunned and even more turned on by his remark about lying between her breasts all night, Evelyn had to ask, "Adam, I know we're married, but I'm still not sure you should be talking to me like that. You know, you being a minister and all."

"So ministers aren't supposed to say sexy things to their wives? Actually, that part about lying between your breasts was kind of quoting scripture. It's also how I feel."

"That's scripture?" Doubt sounded plainly in Evelyn's voice.

"Sure, the Song of Solomon in chapter 1, verse 13 says, 'A bundle of myrrh is my well-beloved unto me; he shall lie all night betwixt my breasts.' We'll have to read the entire book together sometimes. It's full of good stuff like that."

Evelyn could hear the teasing in his voice, but she didn't feel like teasing at all. In fact, she had to get inside the motel and away from him before she gave in to something she might regret later.

Having to clear her throat to get her voice to work, Evelyn said, "I think we'd better get some rest, like you mentioned."

Without another word Adam opened his door and came around the car to open Evelyn's. When they got to her room, he took her room key from his pocket and opened the door. "Let me come in with you to make sure this is to your liking. We didn't check the rooms out when I signed us in earlier."

"I'm sure it's okay," Evelyn hastened to assure him. She didn't think it was a good idea for him to get inside the room with her. The way she felt, she might attack him and throw him to the bed.

"Okay. Just call me if you don't like it. But since this is our honeymoon, I think I should at least get a goodnight kiss."

He was standing close enough for Evelyn to feel the warmth from his body and smell his aftershave. She could feel herself leaning toward him, and couldn't seem to stop herself even if she wanted to. She raised her lips and offered them to him, and he took them in a kiss that she never knew could exist.

As the kiss deepened she raised her arms and slid them around his neck. His arms encircled her waist and drew her tight against his body. She was aware that their bodies fit like perfect puzzle pieces.

She felt all resistance draining from her, and if he hadn't started to slowly draw back she would have pulled him into the room with her.

Adam was obviously shaken. He propped his hands on the doorjamb behind her and lay his head on his arm, pulling in deep gulps of air.

She missed his arms when they were no longer around her. She wanted to step back to him and feel the comfort, the protection, the heat that was there waiting for her.

Finally Adam raised his head, dropped his arms to his side, and just drank her in with his eyes. "Well, there goes my sleep for the night," he said. "Lady, you do pack a punch. I was in deep before that kiss, but I'm going under for the last time, now. I have to go while I still can.

"Goodnight." he said, dropping a soft feather kiss on her lips and walking to the room beside hers. "Be sure and lock all the locks," he reminded her as she disappeared inside.

After locking the door, Evelyn sank into the first chair inside the room. Her legs didn't want to hold her up any longer. She brushed her fingertips across her lips, where she could still feel Adam's kiss. What had she done? She—

The sharp ringing of her cell phone startled her out of her thoughts. "Hello?" she said, seeing Adam's caller I.D.

"I think we forgot something," he said sheepishly.

"What?" Was this a ploy to get into her room?

"What are you going to sleep in tonight?" he asked.

Glancing around for her luggage, Evelyn burst into a peal of laughter, and Adam joined in.

"If you'll open the door, I'll hand your suitcases in to you," he said.

She quickly unlocked the door to find Adam standing there with her suitcase and overnight case in his hands. She swung the door open, and he came in and deposited the luggage against the wall.

"Also, how do you want to handle the morning? Your mom said to not be in any hurry, and Fred said we'd go fishing after lunch. So do you want to sleep in and maybe go to the hotel restaurant for breakfast, or go somewhere else? Or do you just want to sleep in and go to your mom's house later? Or we could just play it by ear."

"Well, I won't sleep longer than eight o'clock under any circumstance, so if you want to, we could agree to be ready by nine and have breakfast here in the restaurant, then go to mom's, if that sounds okay with you."

"Perfect," he said and started toward the door, but turned back to look at her before heading out. After piercing her with those beautiful green eyes, he shook his head and left the room.

EVELYN DIDN'T sleep a wink that night. She lay flat on her back and stared at the dimly lit ceiling all night. Occasionally she glanced at the clock, but didn't even care as she noted each passing hour of sleeplessness.

She'd thought she was in love with Darren Carmichael when they'd gotten married, but not once in their entire marriage had Evelyn been as stimulated as she was tonight after just one real kiss from Adam.

Was what she felt just lust? Or was it the real thing?

She had no doubt that she could spend her life with Adam Singletary, just because he was such a different man than Darren. She couldn't imagine Adam saying something abusive.

But she had to remind herself that sometimes a person's

abusive side didn't show up until after the marriage was well under way. Darren wasn't abusive to start with, either. His abuse didn't start until Evelyn told him she was pregnant. A child didn't fit in with the life he had planned, so he turned into a monster.

No matter where her mind wondered, it always came back to *the kiss*. And she relived every nice thing Adam had ever said or done. She replayed every day they had been together since she'd arrived in Nashville, and she couldn't find a single moment when she'd suspected that he had a nature like Darren.

Was she in love? She was beginning to believe that she was. And if this was love, it was the first time she'd ever been here.

CHAPTER 13

As Evelyn lay and stared at the ceiling, she became aware that the light in the room was changing and realized that dawn had arrived. She glanced at the clock and saw that it was six o'clock.

Had she actually spent the entire night staring into space and thinking about Adam Singletary? Surely she'd dozed off a few times—but, no, she was sure she hadn't slept a wink. This was another first for her.

Well, she might as well get up and get dressed. The sun would be up in a little while, and she knew sleep would escape her then, for sure.

But what was she going to do while she waited on Adam to wake up? Sit and stare at the wall and continue to think about him? She needed to be thinking about what her life was going to be like when they got back to Nashville. But she didn't have a clue as to what she was supposed to think about.

Would she be as out of place with Adam's church friends as she was with Darren's country club friends? For some reason she felt that Adam's friends would be easier to be around. *Please let it be so*, she sent up a quick prayer.

Heading for the bathroom to get a shower, Evelyn decided

to peek out the window to see how light it was, and opened the curtains just in time to see Adam walking past with the *Meridian Star,* the local newspaper, tucked under his arm.

So he was up early, too. Evelyn wondered if he'd gotten any sleep, then chided herself for being silly. Of course he had. She was the only one who was foolish enough to get so caught up in a kiss that she stayed awake all night.

After showering and getting dressed, Evelyn felt the motel room closing in on her and decided to text Adam to see if he would respond. Maybe he'd want to just go ahead and get breakfast and get the day started. *I'm awake and dressed if you want to get started early,* she typed, then sat and stared at the text for several minutes before she sent it. Maybe he just wanted some time alone to read the paper or—what? Maybe pray and study? What did ministers do when they were alone?

Oh for Pete's sake, just send the text! she chided herself, and hit "send." Then sat and stared at her phone, wondering if she'd done the right thing. Maybe he'd gone back to sleep, she thought when he didn't answer her immediately.

A soft knock on the door startled her from her self-doubt. She peeked out the curtains and saw Adam standing at the door with two cups of coffee in his hands. She quickly opened it.

"I know there are coffee pots in the rooms, but I like the coffee from the restaurant better, so I went and got us cups. I hope that's okay," he said, placing the two cups of steaming coffee on the small table before turning to get a better look at Evelyn, who was still holding the open door in her hand.

"Oh. Is it okay if I come in?" he asked.

Feeling like a silly teenager because her heart was already pounding out of her chest, Evelyn quickly closed the door and said, "Well, of course! Thanks for bringing the coffee. Here, let me get—"

"Just sit down here at the table and drink your coffee, Eve. I fixed it like you like it, with one teaspoon of creamer. I'll open the drapes so we'll be exposed to anyone who walks by, and that way we'll have to be good. We have two weeks at this motel, and I just can't see us hiding out from each other for two weeks. Are you okay with that?" With a swoosh of the drawstring, the curtains opened to expose a beautiful sunrise.

Evelyn sat in one of the chairs, wishing she could get past the sudden shyness that seemed to engulf her when Adam was around. "How did you get the coffee that quickly after I sent you the text?" she asked.

"I was over there getting a cup for myself when I got your text, so, since you were awake I decided to bring you a cup and enjoy each other's company over our morning coffee. I sure hope we'll be doing a lot of this when we get back to Nashville. I love my first cup of coffee in the morning, and I will delight in being able to share it with someone I love.

"But you didn't answer my question. Are you okay with me being in your room? If I'm making you uncomfortable, and you do look a little uncomfortable, then I'll just take my coffee and tuck my tail and go back to my dungeon." He ended with his head down and a pout on his beautiful mouth.

Evelyn couldn't stop the laugh that escaped her. "If we ever do have children, they'll be incorrigible if they take after you," she said, then stopped with her hand clamped over her mouth, her eyes huge, not believing what she'd just let slip out.

She'd spent part of her sleepless night imaging what their children would look and be like if they did have any, and the leftover thoughts from her night had escaped in the light of day.

"And they will be as beautiful as their mother," Adam said, acting as if Evelyn wasn't sitting there wishing she could sink through the floor. "They will be so beautiful that we won't be able to discipline them. Anna already proves what beautiful children you can produce." Maybe if he talked long enough, that look of pure horror would disappear from her face. "And you add my own good looks and we'll just have such wonderful, beautiful, incorrigible children that even the teachers won't be able to discipline them," he added, trying to lighten the mood.

Knowing what Adam was doing, and appreciating it, Evelyn said, "Adam—"

"Eve, drink your coffee and let's talk about the day ahead."

"Are you going to let me finish a sentence this morning?" Evelyn asked, feeling some of her embarrassment disappear to be replaced by a little irritation.

"Nope. Not if you're going to try and take back something that's just made my day. What you said lets me know you've been thinking about us long-term, and that makes me absolutely happy. Did you sleep well last night? Was the bed comfortable?" he asked, trying to change the subject.

But for Evelyn, remembering the night before didn't help at all. And as tempting as it was, she just couldn't bring herself to lie to Adam. "The bed is wonderfully comfortable. But I didn't sleep very well," she said, leaving out the "not at all" part. "Did you sleep well?"

"I didn't sleep a wink. I didn't doze off one single time. I spent the night staring at the ceiling and thinking about you. About us. I was too wired to sleep. So I'm kind of glad you didn't sleep that well, either. Maybe—although I know you won't admit it—maybe you thought about me a little," Adam said, and sipped his coffee.

Just watching his lips form the sipping motion for the coffee sent Evelyn into a hot flash. *Get a grip*! she mentally yelled at herself.

"I did think of you some," she felt compelled to admit.

"What did you think about? Was it the kiss? Did you wonder if it really was as good as it seemed? That's what I was thinking about. Do you want to try it again to see if it really was that good?"

"Adam, we need to go get breakfast!" Evelyn said, picking up her purse. *And get out of this room before—*

But before she could finish that thought Adam had moved close to her and drawn her into his arms. "See, we're right in front of the open window, so anybody walking past can see us. We have the world as our chaperone."

As Evelyn glanced at the window, an older man stopped and was looking in.

"Adam! That man is watching us," Evelyn said, trying to push away from him.

"Good. Let's give him something to see." He lowered his lips to hers and took her mouth in a slow, sensuous kiss. Giving in to the overpowering feelings that engulfed her, Evelyn's arms crept up around his neck.

When Adam finally lifted his mouth from hers, she felt too dazed to open her eyes. But a light pecking on glass caused her eyes to fly open, and she and Adam looked toward the window.

The old man was grinning from ear to ear. He gave them two thumbs up before shuffling on down the walkway.

"See, we did our good deed for the day," Adam said. "He'll feel young and happy for the rest of the day."

"But you're right. We'd better get out of here and get in a more public place. Let's go get breakfast."

THEY'D FINISHED breakfast and were on the way to her mom's house when Evelyn's cell phone rang. Seeing Julie's caller ID, she said, "Oh, it's Julie. I hope everything's okay. Hello?" She was surprised to hear Jim's voice when she answered the phone. "Jim? What's wrong? Is Julie okay?"

"Julie's fine, Eve, but I don't have good news—" he paused, not sure how to break the news, but Evelyn waited. Finally Jim said, "Eve, I hate to have to be the one to tell you this, but the store burned down last night. Nothing was saved! It's a total loss."

Stunned, Evelyn sat and stared at her phone as tears filled her eyes.

"What?" Adam asked. "Eve, what's wrong?" When she didn't answer, Adam reached for her phone and said, "Jim, what's going on?"

Jim repeated to Adam what he'd told Evelyn.

"Do we know how the fire started?" Adam asked.

"The fire chief said they weren't sure, but they suspect foul play."

"You mean arson?" Adam asked.

CHAPTER 14

"NO!" EVELYN ERUPTED FROM HER STUPOR. "PLEASE don't tell me someone deliberately burned down my business," she said, giving Adam a pleading look.

"They don't know for sure," Jim repeated. "But that's what the fire chief thinks."

Adam said a few more words, then hung up. "What do you want to do?" he asked, taking Evelyn's balled fist into his large hand, trying to unclamp her fingers.

Little by little she allowed her fingers to relax and be held in Adam's supporting hand. "We'll have to go back, Adam. I have to go back and see for myself. I need to talk to Julie and see if anyone suspicious has been in the store."

"Could Darren have stooped this low to get revenge?"

"I don't doubt that he might want to, but I doubt he did it himself. He may have hired someone to do it, but I can't see him stooping low enough to do his own dirty work."

"So do you want to leave today?" he asked.

"If we leave at noon, we can be back in Nashville by six or seven o'clock. So, yes, if you don't mind, I'd like to go back today so I can start the day early in the morning."

"If the place is destroyed, you won't be able to go on the

property until the authorities are finished checking out all evidence and leads," Adam reminded. "Plus, we can't afford to forget the thugs who shot into your apartment. It might have been one of them who did the deed. And if we go back, we'll just be taking you back into danger."

Sucking in a quick breath, Evelyn covered her face with her hands and said, "I had totally forgotten about those guys! That makes more sense than Darren. But I'm not going to hide from whoever did it! I need to be there to ask and answer questions."

"Okay, if that's what you want, we can pick up Anna and Mangy and go back to the motel for our luggage."

They rode in silence for a few minutes, then Evelyn said, "I was looking forward to spending Thanksgiving with mom, but now that's ruined."

A plan slowly developed in Adam's mind, but they reached the house before he had time to mention it to Evelyn.

As they pulled into the driveway Anna and Mangy ran around the corner of the house to meet them.

"Mommy! Adam!" Anna called, hurling herself into Adam's arms because he was the closest. Evelyn's heart lurched to see the joy on Anna's little face when Adam lifted her up over his head and spun her around before lowering her into his arms and hugging her.

"I missed you," Anna said, giving Adam a smacking kiss right on the lips.

Adam laughed out loud and said, "I missed you too, Squirt!"

Mangy was jumping around and barking because he wanted some of the attention, so Adam stood Anna down and patted Mangy on the head. "And I missed you, too, you ugly dog!"

Anna ran to Evelyn, and Evelyn gathered her closely in a tight hug. Should she take Anna back to Nashville, now? What if she was taking her back into a dangerous situation? What were these people capable of besides burning down a building?

Just then Fred and Sara came out the front door. "What's all the commotion?" Sara asked. "You're going to have my neighbors calling the cops, you're making so much noise."

"Hi, Mom. Fred. We need to go inside. We have some bad news," Evelyn said, heading toward her mom.

Concern flashed across her mom's face, but nobody said a word until they were all gathered in the living room.

"What in the world is going on?" Sara asked, watching Evelyn's face.

"Mom," Evelyn said, fighting her tears, "We have to go back to Nashville today. Someone has burned my store down." Just saying the words out loud brought the reality home, and Evelyn sat on the couch and buried her face in her hands and let the tears flow.

The room remained in a stunned silence for a moment before Adam sat on the couch beside Evelyn and pulled her to him.

"I'll get a glass of water and a cold bath cloth for her," Sara said, leaving the room.

Fred sat in the recliner beside the window. Anna perched on the edge of the couch on the opposite side of Evelyn and leaned against her, unsure how to react at seeing her mother cry so hard.

Sara hurried back to the room and set the glass of water on the coffee table and laid the bath cloth beside it, then sat in the recliner beside Fred's.

Evelyn reached for the bath cloth and covered her face with it. The cold cloth helped her to come out of her crying jag. Then she took a drink of the water.

"I'm sorry to just crumble like that," she apologized to the room.

"Now, don't you dare start that racket," Sara scolded. "You've been through too much in the past two years. You deserve a good cry. Now Adam, while she pulls herself together, please tell us what's going on."

Adam explained about the phone call they'd gotten. "The fire chief and the Nashville police department are checking it out, but haven't confirmed the cause of the fire yet. But Jim said they suspect arson. Has Eve told you about the drive-by shooting at her apartment a few days ago?"

"Adam!" Evelyn warned, but it was too late.

"Come again?" Sara said, sliding to the edge of the recliner seat. "Evelyn Nicole Tew Carmichael Singletary! I *knew* you were holding out on me! Haven't you learned in your twenty-eight years of being my child that I *will always* find out your secrets? Why in the hell haven't you told me about this?"

Sara suddenly clamped her hands over her mouth, realizing she had cursed in front of a minister and her grandchild. But it was done and she couldn't take it back, so she continued, "Will someone please tell me what's going on with you two?"

Evelyn looked at Adam and, with a slight smile, said, "Go ahead, you've let the cat halfway out of the bag, so you might as well go ahead and let it all out."

So Adam told Sara and Fred everything.

He covered the dangerous, small apartment where Evelyn had been living. *Kind of overkill*, Evelyn thought. He told them about Darren showing up and threatening to try to take Anna and how he, Adam, had stepped in and told Darren that he was Evelyn's fiancé, and how he'd persuaded Evelyn to marry him for convenience sake. *Hounded me is more like it*, Evelyn thought. And he told them about the huge house he was living in, and that he hoped that someday their marriage would be for real, because he was in love with her and would always love her.

Sara and Fred had sat quietly during Adam's disclosure, but, at that point Fred looked at Sara and said, "I told you the man was smitten with her!"

"You're absolutely correct," Adam said. "'Smitten' is the perfect word for how I feel about Eve, and I'm totally in love with Anna, too." At which point Anna went to him and crawled into his lap.

"Eve is devastated that we won't be able to have Thanksgiving with you all, but I have an idea that I'd like to run by you. Thanksgiving is almost two weeks away, so that will probably give the authorities enough time to come to some kind of conclusion about the fire, and maybe things will have settled down a little by then. Why don't you two come to Nashville for Thanksgiving? As I said, the house is big enough for several families, so that won't be a problem. In fact, you can come and stay as long as you'd like.

"Nashville has some wonderful tourist attractions. It's known as Music City, but there are a lot of things going on that don't include music. There are art museums, the Tennessee Museum downtown that features over sixty thousand square feet of permanent exhibits and a ten thousand square foot changing exhibition hall, there are historic houses to see, and the list goes on. So what do you say? Come on up for a visit. I'm sure it would take Eve's mind off her store if you'd come." Okay, he admitted to himself that the last was just a little bit of manipulation on his part, but maybe it would work.

Sara and Fred looked at each other with their eyebrows lifted, but neither said a word until they both nodded their heads as if reading each other's minds. Then Sara said, "Okay, it's done. We'll just plan on that. And I have an idea of my own. Why don't you leave Anna and Mangy with Fred and me, and we'll bring them home at Thanksgiving. That way you two will be able to pursue all the business you need to take care of.

"And I'm not just talking about the store, Eve. You were married to a jerk. I'm pretty sure he was your first experience with sex. So all you're familiar with in a man is a jerk wad. Open your heart, girl, and give Adam a chance. He's a good man. You know I can sense these things. He's a good man, I repeat!

"Go home, and the first thing you do is get in bed and the

two of you get rid of some of your pent-up anxieties so you can be more relaxed and figure out who's trying to hurt you."

"Where's that old-fashioned mom you told me about? I'm sure not seeing her in this room," Adam said teasingly to Evelyn.

"You called me old-fashioned?" Sara asked, actually looking insulted.

Before Evelyn could defend herself Anna jumped up from the couch and stood in front of her. "Please, Mom! Let me and Mangy stay with Gramma and Gramps."

"Oh, it's already Gramps?" Evelyn asked, looking at Fred.

"Yep! She came up with that on her own, I'm happy to say," Fred answered.

"I think that's an excellent idea, considering the situation we may be going back into," Adam said, "but it's your decision."

"Please, please, puleeze!" Anna begged, jumping up and down.

Unsure of what waited for them back in Nashville, Evelyn gave in. "Okay, I think that's a good idea," she said to Anna, who grabbed her around the neck and hugged her.

"Thanks, Mom and Fred," Evelyn continued after Anna let her go. Then the fact that her mom and Fred would be in Nashville for Thanksgiving sank into her mind, and she was suddenly excited about it. A big smile broke across her face.

"You're really coming to Nashville?" she asked, almost wanting to jump up and down like Anna. "You're going to love Adam's house! It's huge, like he said, and beautiful. I can't wait for you to see it."

"It's *our* house, now, Mommy," Anna spoke up. "It Adam's and yours and Mangy's and my house! Right, Adam?" She looked at Adam for confirmation.

"That's right, Squirt. It's our house, and you have to keep helping me remind your mommy about that. But I guess we need to head back to Nashville, if we want to get there before midnight," Adam said, realizing they'd taken more time than they'd meant to.

"I'm ready to get back and follow Sara's orders," he said, his eyes twinkling at Evelyn. "We have to obey your parent—you know that's Biblical, Eve."

"Mom, I fear you've created a bigger monster than I already had," Evelyn said, rolling her eyes at Adam.

"Don't worry, honey, I know you can handle any size monster you need to," Sara said, outright laughing at her daughter's disgruntled look.

CHAPTER 15

By one o'clock Adam and Evelyn were on the interstate headed back to Nashville.

"Since we won't have to stop so often with Anna and Mangy, and if traffic isn't horrible, we'll probably be able to make it home around seven or so," Adam said.

"That's what I'd figured," Evelyn said, but didn't offer any other conversation.

Home. The thought of just her and Adam going into that huge house to spend the night alone sent quivers of anxiety through Evelyn. She knew Adam would respect his word and not try to force himself on her, but it was herself she was worried about, not him.

For some reason, being in the house alone was different than being next door to him in the motel. Being in the house seemed more intimate.

But being alone with him in the motel room had made it perfectly clear to Evelyn that she was greatly tempted by Adam Singletary. More tempted than she'd ever been by any other man. And when he'd kissed her, she was putty in his hands.

She didn't like feeling weak. Weakness was something she'd always fought against. But when he wrapped her up in his arms, her fight abandoned her and left her feeling vulnerable and needy.

Well, she *was* needy! She needed to be held. She needed to be told she was desirable, which Adam did a good job of, but she needed that in context with actions, not just words. She needed to know she was loved.

"I guess we need to go to church next Sunday." Adam interrupted her wayward thoughts. "By then the congregation will know we're back in town, although I don't aim to go back on the job until my two weeks are up. It's been a long time since I've taken any days off, so I plan to enjoy them. But I need to introduce you as my new wife."

"That brings up something that's been nagging at me, Adam. What are the people going to say about you marrying a fat woman?"

Adam took his eyes off the road to look at Evelyn as if she'd lost her senses. "I haven't even considered that that subject would come up. I can't see why anybody would have a say about what size woman I marry. Plus, I haven't seen one solitary woman in several years who doesn't think she's fat. I've even heard Sally Johnson talk about needing to lose weight, as tall and thin as she is."

"I won't deny that I felt a spark of interest between us that first day when I went to church and saw you," Evelyn said. "And I don't think you're pretending to be interested in me. But I don't understand why. I would think that a man as handsome as you are would be looking for the typical model-thin woman to be by your side."

"Now, that's just insulting to me and all the other men in the world who appreciate a well-padded woman, Eve! I find women your size to be very desirable, but I've never found a woman of any size that thrilled me down to my soul like you do.

"Attraction is an individual perception. Thank God for that!

If we all were attracted to the same kind of person, there would be a lot of lonely people out there."

"I know all that. It's just that I started dieting when I was in my early teens, and continued until right after Anna was born. I wasn't real thin when I met Darren, but I was thin enough that he seemed to be attracted to me. But when I started gaining weight after Anna was born, he started saying some really horrible things to me and calling me really hurtful names, so he pretty much destroyed my self-confidence. I've been working on getting it back, because my logical mind knows that beauty really does come in all sizes. That's why I wanted to open a boutique with beautiful larger size clothes."

"Look, Darren has already proven what a waste of good air he is, so you need to block out any and everything he's ever said to you. Because you're a very beautiful, sexy, desirable woman, Evelyn Nicole Singletary! You can take my word for that. But from now on, I'm going to do my best to remind you of it several times a day."

"Then it will look like you're just saying stuff to make me feel better," Evelyn said.

"Will it work?"

"Probably so," she answered, with a giggle that she tried to stifle before it slipped out. "But what about the gluttony thing? I've heard some people believe people are fat because they're gluttonous and eat too much. And I've heard that gluttony is a sin."

"The word 'gluttony' isn't even in the Bible. The word 'glutton' is mentioned two times in the Old Testament, and that's talking about a lifestyle. The word 'gluttonous' is only mentioned two times in the New Testament, and that's when Jesus is saying that others have called him gluttonous and a winebibber because he ate meat and drank wine. I really don't mind being compared to Jesus, do you?"

"No. Wow. I never knew that."

"Plus," Adam continued, "Scripture says that the Lord doesn't see mankind as mankind sees each other. He says that man looks on the outward appearance, but the Lord looks at the heart. Scripture also says that we shouldn't compare ourselves among ourselves."

"And that's exactly what women do!" Evelyn said. "Wow, you know a lot about this subject."

"Well, a few years ago several women in the congregation decided that the entire church needed to go on a diet and that we needed to have folks from a fairly well-known 'religious' diet program come in and show us all how to pray ourselves slim and 'healthy.'

"I was totally against this for several reasons. My cousin had anorexia when she was in her teens, and I know how devastating that can be to a person. I knew that if mothers, aunts, grandmothers etc. were obsessing over losing weight, that would cause our young girls and boys to think about it more. And who knows how many other teens—and adults, for that matter—would head down that long road of eating disorders.

"So I gave a fairly point-blank sermon about it, and after that the talk died down. I won't dictate to my congregation how they should handle things like that, but I will let them know in no uncertain terms how I feel about it.

"There's a lot more I could go into, but I'll just say that nowhere in the Bible does it say that it's a sin to be fat, or thin, or short or tall. The perfect body style isn't mentioned in the Word."

"This is so interesting!" Evelyn said. "Have you ever heard of the Venus of Willendorf?"

"No, I don't think I have," Adam said.

"She's one of the earliest man-carved images of the body. She was found in 1908 by an archeologist near the town of Willendorf in Austria, but nobody knows who she is or what her purpose was supposed to have been.

"She's a very fat, nude statue that fits in the palm of the hand. She doesn't have a face, but the rest of her body is very distinct. I've always wished she could be traced back to the original Eve."

"Maybe one day they will do just that!" Adam said. "But in the meantime, you are my Eve, and I think you're the most beautiful woman in the world."

"Oh, puleeze!" Evelyn knew she sounded like Anna with that remark, but she couldn't help herself."

"I see I have my work cut out for me," Adam said, reaching over and taking Evelyn's hand and holding on to it.

THEY STOPPED in Birmingham, filled the car up with gas, and got coffee and a snack. It was getting close to four o'clock, and cloudy, so darkness wasn't that far away.

As they settled back into the car and headed north on I-65 to Nashville, Evelyn's nervousness came back in full force. The oncoming night didn't help any.

What were the authorities going to find out about her store? And when would she know? Would her insurance pay enough for her to start another business? She didn't want to just sit at home and do nothing. Especially now that they were living with Adam. She wanted to be independent. If things didn't work out with Adam, she wanted to be able to support herself and Anna.

"What's wrong, Eve? You seem nervous all of a sudden," Adam said. "Do you want to talk about it?"

"I'm just wondering about the situation with the store," she said. "I have so many questions and no answers, at this point."

"The answers will come. Just try to relax and wait. I know that's hard, but there really isn't any way you can hurry this type of thing along.

"For now, just think about Thanksgiving and your mom and Fred being here. Let's talk about some of the places we'll take them to see. Tell me what your mom is interested in," Adam encouraged.

So for the rest of the trip they talked and planned for the upcoming visit, and Evelyn felt herself slowly relaxing and listening to Adam tell of all the interesting places in and around Nashville that they could visit.

And in what seemed like no time at all, Evelyn saw the lights of Nashville appear in the near distance.

CHAPTER 16

THREE DAYS HAD PASSED SINCE ADAM AND EVELYN HAD arrived back in Nashville. Adam was upstairs in his office making a few calls, and Evelyn was downstairs in the large library that Mrs. Smith had left stocked with books.

The day was perfect for curling up with a good book. A slow rain fell, and the occasional raindrop landed on the windowpane and slowly curled its way downward. It was, after all, November, and the weather was letting everyone know that winter was here to stay for a while. A cold, brisk wind whipped around the corners of the house, causing a low, sad moan to occasionally interrupt the silence.

Evelyn had pulled a book from the shelf with all intention of trying to read it, but it lay unopened in her lap because the day had her missing Anna and her mom. She couldn't wait for next Wednesday, when they'd get here.

She hadn't bothered to turn on the lights in the room when she came in, and since she had sat down the clouds had thickened and the room had gotten darker. She needed to get up and turn on the lights if she was going to read, but she just wasn't in the mood to move.

There was no official word on what or who had caused the

fire that burned her store down. She and Adam had gone to the site the morning after they'd gotten back into Nashville, but just as Adam had suspected, the area was marked off with yellow police ribbon and nobody was supposed to cross it.

The police didn't think it was the people connected with the drugs and drive-by shootings at her apartment, because they had kept apartment 12C under surveillance for several days and had finally busted the residents for making methamphetamine. The police had questioned them about the shooting, but were convinced the drive-by was not related to the meth lab. The police suspected the drive-by shooting had been an initiation into one of the local gangs, but were still investigating the incident. The police were pretty convinced that the meth makers were not the arsonists. Which pointed back to Darren.

Evelyn became aware of female voices just before two women stepped into the dimly lit library. They had to be Amy Moore and Betty Lucas, the two women who came once a week and cleaned the house. They must have had a key, because Evelyn hadn't heard them knock. Adam's and her car were in the garage, so these two ladies might not know they were back from their trip and had just let themselves in. They weren't trying to keep their voices low, so apparently they thought they had the house to themselves.

"I mean," Betty was saying, "I just can't understand why Pastor Adam would marry a fat woman when we've all introduced him to perfectly normal-sized young women."

"I know," Amy joined in. "Doesn't he know that not taking care of your body and letting yourself go like that is a sin? Maybe she's pregnant. You know, she does have that little girl, and she wasn't even married, as far as I know."

"Well, I just can't figure it out," Betty said. "But I guess we need to get started. I need to be home before the kids get off the school bus." And she reached over and flipped on the light switch.

Their eyes fell on Evelyn at the same time. Both of their mouths dropped open as each woman stared at Evelyn as if she was an apparition sitting in the recliner.

"Hello, ladies," Evelyn said, maintaining a much cooler outer countenance than she felt inside. "I guess you didn't know that Adam and I had gotten back into town. I would like to throw my two cents' worth into the conversation that you were just having—about me. You see," she said, pulling from the conversation that she and Adam had had on the trip home, "the scriptures don't mention a thing about fat being a sin, but scripture does say a whole lot about gossip. Maybe you two need to spend more time reading your Bibles instead of just talking about what you think it says."

"Well, I never!" Amy said, and turned and left the room with Betty close on her heels.

Somewhere in another part of the house, probably the kitchen, Evelyn heard the two women talking to Adam. She couldn't understand what was being said. But soon Adam came to the library where Evelyn still sat.

"So this is where you are! I couldn't find you anywhere. Did you meet Amy and Betty? Did you let them in? I didn't hear the doorbell."

"Apparently they didn't know we were back, so they must have let themselves in," Evelyn answered. Should she tell him what had just happened? Or should she just let it pass and maybe it would settle down after folks got tired of gossiping about her?

"Why don't we go to Cracker Barrel and get lunch while they clean the house? That way we'll be out of the house and they can clean faster."

And have plenty of freedom to trash me, Evelyn thought. "Okay, that sounds good," she said. She needed to get out of the house and clear her mind. She didn't know what was wrong with her today. Maybe it was just the weather—although she normally liked rainy days.

Evelyn was quiet as Adam drove to the restaurant, and hoped he wouldn't notice. But her luck didn't hold for long.

"Are you okay? You sure are quiet," he said.

"I think I'm just missing Anna and Mangy," she answered, honestly. She really did miss them.

"I know. I miss them, too, but in just a few days they'll be here." He reached over and squeezed her hand. "Eve, did something happen between you and the two women at the house? I wanted to introduce you to them, but they said they'd had the honor. Betty had a very snarky look on her face, and Amy looked to be close to tears."

Okay, there goes my good intentions on this, Evelyn thought. Then she told him everything that had happened, including her telling them that they needed to read their Bibles.

She was expecting anything except the loud laugh that exploded from Adam. "You actually told them that?" he asked, unbelief in his voice. "Betty teaches the adult Sunday School class, and Amy teaches a children's Sunday School class."

"See, Adam! I told you I wasn't minister's wife material. I've already made enemies with two of the church members, and I totally get the feeling that Sally Johnson doesn't like me. So other than Julie and Jim, nobody from the church that I've met likes me. I think you've made a big mistake!

"But know this. I'm not sure how much crap you think I should take, as a Christian and or as a minister's wife, but I refuse to sit and listen to someone put me down. Been there and done that! And after Darren, I promised myself that I would never allow that again!"

Adam had pulled into the Cracker Barrel parking lot and parked the car while Evelyn was talking. Now he turned and placed his arm on the back of her seat and looked at her with a huge grin on his face.

"You, my dear wife, are exactly what this church needs! You

don't come with the preprogrammed self-righteous, holier-than-thou attitude that so many church members adopt over their years of being Christians.

"You're just you. You're open and honest and tell it like it is. And yet you have a heart so full of love that it gleams from your beautiful eyes. I've seen you look at people and I watch them respond to the look in your eyes. They're drawn to you. Well, most of them," he added with another laugh.

"People like the women we've just discussed need you as an example. Now, I want you to stop worrying about not being a good minister's wife. All you have to do is be yourself, and before you know it you'll have the entire congregation wrapped around your little finger."

Again, he laughed. "I can't believe you told them to read their Bibles! What a jewel you are. Oh, I don't think I've made a mistake, my Eve, I think I've just added life to my church."

"Adam!" Evelyn exclaimed. "That's Darren coming out of the restaurant talking to that sleazy looking guy! And they're headed right toward us!"

"Just be still and don't look at them," Adam said. "Maybe they'll come by us and we can hear a little of what they're saying."

"I think that's his BMW parked beside you," Evelyn said, scooting lower in her seat. She kept her eyes on her lap and Adam kept his head tilted, watching the men approach through the rearview mirror.

Sure enough, since Darren had backed into his parking space, he stopped just outside of Adam's door, with his back to Adam. But instead of getting in his car he stood facing the man on the other side of the car and said, "I don't care where they are. I plan to find them. I thought hiring you to burn down the store would flush her out, but I haven't seen a sign of her, and I've sat and watched that chunk of ashes ever since the store went up in flames. I will have my daughter back, for no other reason than spite." Then the two got in the car and pulled out of the parking space.

Adam quickly took a pen from the console of his car and wrote the BMW's license plate number on the palm of his hand, then took his cell phone and called Detective Greer, who was in charge of the case.

"I think we have our arsonist," he said when the detective answered. He told the detective what he and Evelyn had heard, and Darren's name. "It's a Mississippi license plate," Adam added before signing off.

"Wow! What a great coincidence," Evelyn said after taking a deep, calming breath.

"Personally, I call things like this a 'God Thing,'" Adam said. "This was just meant to be. I hadn't even thought about coming here for lunch until I found you in the library. I came downstairs to see if you wanted us to make a sandwich for lunch. But we landed here instead. And just in time for those two to walk out of the restaurant. If we'd been one minute later or earlier, we wouldn't have heard Darren's admission of what they'd done."

Adam reached over and took Evelyn's hand and held it, idly stroking his thumb in small circles on the back of her hand, causing ripples of butterflies to flutter in her stomach.

She glanced at his profile and realized that he didn't even know what he was doing. He was lost in thought, and this act of reaching out and connecting was as natural as breathing for him. And she knew, in that instant, that Adam Singletary was absolutely nothing like Darren Carmichael.

Slowly, still watching Adam, Evelyn turned her hand over and laced her fingers with his. For a moment nothing happened, but gradually it dawned on Adam what she'd done and he snapped out of his deep thoughts. Not moving his hand except to tighten his grip, he turned to look into Evelyn's eyes. What she saw churned her entire being. Never had she *ever* been looked at with so much love.

"I've heard you talk about Darren, and I witnessed his actions in your apartment that day, but I didn't really *get it* until I heard the hate in his voice just now. That man has some deep-seated problems. Why would he hate you so much just because you divorced him?"

"Because when I got fat and divorced him and didn't stay and play his games, I became an embarrassment to him. He felt like all his friends thought he was a failure because his marriage had failed. So it became his mission to make sure everyone who knew us as a couple understood that it was all my fault. And now, I've taken his precious daughter out of the state of Mississippi and defied his orders not to, so in his mind he's forced to take Anna from me to prove what a good guy he is. And the sad thing is, most of his friends believe him because they've never seen his abusive side. To them he's the best thing that ever walked on God's green earth."

The rain had drizzled out, and the sun was trying to peek through the clouds.

"Do you want to still grab lunch?" Adam asked.

"Sure," Evelyn said. "Now that we know who burned down my shop, I'm feeling a lot better!"

"I think I feel worse," Adam said. "It's almost like it's more personal now. And I heard the anger and hatred and determination in his voice. I don't think the drug dealers would be as scary as he is."

"Well, I've seen a good many of his tantrums, and most of them have been pointed at me, so I guess I'm just hardened to them. He really doesn't bother me that much. But I do appreciate your concern," Evelyn said. "I'm thankful Anna is with Mom, though, and not in Nashville, since he's here. I'm sure that if he'd seen us on the street he would have tried to snatch Anna and take her back to Mississippi. He thinks he's above the law and that he can buy off anybody he needs to. That's the way he was raised."

During the conversation Evelyn had not lost awareness that their hands were still clasped, and how wonderful it felt just to have the touch of someone who loved you and to know that you loved them. "Oh!" she exclaimed, snatching her hand from Adam's. She'd suspected that she was growing to love Adam, but the thought had never come into her knowledge so fixed and powerfully as it just had.

"What's wrong? Did I hurt you?" Adam asked. Taking her hand and looking for damage on it, but finding none, he lifted it to his mouth and kissed the back, then the palm.

Evelyn tried to pull her hand away again, and to open the door. She had to get out of this car before she swooned and made a fool of herself.

But Adam held on to her hand and said, "Nope. You're not going anywhere until you tell me what that was all about. We've been holding hands for several minutes, and all of a sudden you act as if I'd bitten you. What's going on, Eve?" Concern had Adam's facial features drawn tight, and his eyes pleaded with her to tell him the problem.

"Adam, it really wasn't anything," she tried to explain. "I just had a startling realization, that's all."

"Under the circumstances, don't you think I deserve to know?" he asked.

"It has nothing to do with the Darren circumstances," Evelyn answered.

"Then what? Just tell me so we can go get lunch. I'm beginning to be hungry."

Why not just tell him? Evelyn wondered. He'd told her many times that he loved her. It didn't have to mean a lifetime commitment if they didn't want it to. Did it?

"Eve, I'm waiting."

"Now, don't throw this way out of proportion," Evelyn warned. "But I just realized that I love you."

All movement stopped in the car. It was as if neither of the people were breathing. Just when Evelyn didn't think she could take the suspense any longer, Adam said, "Say it again, Eve. Say it without the falderal surrounding it."

Looking into his beautiful green eyes and seeing her future there, Evelyn said, "I love you, Adam."

He placed his large hands on each side of her face and gazed into her amber eyes. The sun burst from behind the clouds and highlighted the red streaks in her dark brown hair, giving a halo effect. As he lowered his lips to hers, he knew without a doubt that he had truly found his Eve.

CHAPTER 17

Aftrer finishing their meal, Adam and Evelyn were headed home when his cell phone rang. "Adam Singletary," he said without taking his eyes off the street to check the caller ID. After listening intently, he said, "Okay, I'll be there as soon as I can."

Evelyn saw the tight set of Adam's mouth and asked, "What's wrong?"

"Danny Shirley is at it again. Every few months he gets drunk and starts knocking Linda around. She calls the police and they come out and talk to Danny, but when it comes time to file charges Linda won't go through with it. This has been going on for years. He's never hurt her badly enough for her to go to the hospital, but she does come to church with bruises on her face and arms. Then when the cops leave and he sobers up a little, they call me to come to their house and counsel them, and we all know that nothing is going to change. I just wish Linda would go ahead and file charges so Danny could spend a few nights in jail. Maybe that might jar him into stopping his abuse."

"Are we going over there now?" Evelyn asked.

"Well, I was going to take you home, then go over. I didn't

think you'd want to go."

"I think I do. Maybe if a woman who's been through this talks to her, it might make a difference."

"Darren didn't physically hit you, did he?"

"No, but abuse is abuse. Whether it's the body that's bruised or the soul, the person is still hurt."

After giving Evelyn a mysterious smile, Adam took the first left street and headed into a part of town where the houses were small and close together, but the streets and yards were well-manicured and clean.

Soon he pulled into a driveway beside a big dually pickup truck. The yard would need to be groomed soon, but it wasn't overgrown. The house had a fresh coat of white paint and looked neat and well-kept.

The door opened before Adam and Evelyn had made it to the steps that led to the porch, and a tiny, middle-aged woman stepped out onto the porch.

Is this the woman who's being abused? Evelyn wondered. The woman didn't look that hurt, but as they got closer she could see dark bruises beginning to show on the woman's arms and one on her cheek.

"Hi, Linda," Adam said, going up the steps to the woman who stepped into his arms, welcoming his warm hug. "Linda, this is Eve, my new wife." He drew Evelyn close to his side.

"Adam and Eve?" Linda asked, a huge smile spreading across her face. "Isn't that just perfect!" She reached out and pulled Eve to her in a tight hug. "I'm so happy Adam has found someone! Now maybe all of us women in the church will stop harassing him about getting married."

"LINDA!" A gruff voice bellowed from inside the house. "WHO'RE YOU JABBERING WITH?"

"Okay, let's get this over with," Adam said, opening the door and letting the two women go in before him.

"Preacher?" The man looked to be a good bit older than

Linda. He was huge and looked like a former wrestler.

Surely not! was the first thing that popped into Evelyn's mind. How could a woman so tiny withstand the power of a man this big? She was instantly angry at the very thought.

"Hello, Danny," Adam said. "You been knocking Linda around again?"

"That's what she claims, Preacher, but I can't for the life of me remember doing anything like that. You know I love my wife. And she knows I love her. I don't know why she keeps saying I'm mean to her."

"So now you're forgetting about things you're doing, or are you just lying to save face with me?"

Evelyn saw the first flash of anger pass quickly through the man's eyes before it disappeared. She recognized the signs. She'd done a lot of research on abuse after Darren had started with her, and she'd learned to recognize the signs that he was going to get mean.

But before Danny could answer, Adam pulled Evelyn forward and said, "This is my new wife, Eve. I want you to be nice around her, okay? Don't start your normal cursing and carrying on."

So Adam had seen the signs, too.

"Adam and Eve?" Danny asked, disbelief on his face. "Well, I'll be da—durned if I haven't woke up in the Garden of Eden! Linda, why don't you get Eve here a nice red apple? She's got a tempting body, but she might need some fruit to finish Preacher off."

"Now, Danny," Linda said, quietly. It was apparent that she didn't want to do anything to get him started again.

"Ah, hell, woman, don't 'now, Danny' me. This is my house and I'll say what I want to say to who I want to say it to. Understand?"

"Or what?" Evelyn couldn't believe she'd jumped right in the middle of this situation. "Are you going to slap her around some more? Have you looked in the mirror lately? You're a frigging giant! How could you hit someone as small and frail as your wife? You're nothing but a bully—you're not a man.

"You want to hit someone, why don't you have a go at me? Or am I too big for you? Maybe you're afraid of a large woman. I might hurt you, so you'll just pound on the little ones. Is that the way it is?"

"Eve—" Adam warned.

Suddenly Danny threw his head back and roared with laughter. "Preacher, you've got yourself a real woman, there! Linda, if you'd ever stand up for yourself like Eve here, I probably wouldn't ever hit you."

"Oh, bull crap!" Evelyn said, not even looking around to see if Adam had passed out at her language. "I've been in an abusive situation, and standing up to my bully husband just made him worse. And it would make you worse, too. But you know what I did? I left the SOB! I packed my clothes and walked out on him. Where would you be if Linda did that to you? She needs to, you know."

Suddenly the big man looked defeated. "I couldn't live without my Linda," he said, with what looked like tears coming to his eyes. "I know she should leave me, but she might as well just shoot me in the head, because I'd be dead, either way."

"Then why don't you act like it?" Evelyn said. "Because one day she may just decide she's had enough."

"You wouldn't ever leave me, would you?" He turned his pleading eyes to Linda.

Typical abusive behavior! Evelyn thought angrily. Act out their anger, then repent and say they'll never do it again.

"Danny, I've had a suitcase packed and stored in the attic for two years. I've gotten as far as the front door with it a couple of times, and one day, if you keep on, I'm not going to stop at the front door. I'll keep going."

The man looked as if someone had slapped him upside the

head. He sat with a stunned look on his face before finally looking at Adam.

"Preacher, tell me again where I can go to them Triple A meetings," he said. "I heard Ron Smith got religion and started going to one of them meetings. Hell, if he can sober up, I know I can. We used to be real close friends. We'd get drunk and raise all kinds of hell." A smile of remembered "good times" briefly crossed his face.

"It's AA meetings, Alcoholics Anonymous, and if you're serious, I'll take you to your first one," Adam said.

"I'm serious, Preacher. Your woman has made me look at myself a little differently. I mean, I *am* a big brute, and my Linda is just a little bitty woman. I should never lay a hand on her. And sober, I wouldn't, but the booze does it to me every time, even though I tell myself when I start to drink that I'm not going to hurt her. But I always do.

"And now that I know I've come so close to losing her, I know I'd better straighten my act up. So where are the meetings?"

"We have a meeting in our church tonight. One of our church members is an alcoholic, and he'll be there."

"Would that member be Ron? Linda said he goes to your church."

"I can't tell you who goes to the meetings, because they're anonymous," Adam said. "But yes, he goes to the church where I'm pastor."

"Well, I'll be da—durned! Maybe I'll sober up and start going to church again. I grew up in church, but haven't been in a long time. I kind of got turned off with some of the preachers and stopped going. I guess if my Linda likes your preaching so much, I might be able to stand it."

Evelyn was amazed to see Linda walk over and crawl into the big man's lap and place a kiss on his cheek. "I promise you, you'll enjoy Pastor Adam's sermons. He's different than any minister I've ever heard. He's real, and doesn't try to put on a 'holier than thou' attitude."

"Okay, I'll try it, but if I decide to miss a Sunday every now and then, don't start nagging on me."

Linda giggled like a schoolgirl. "Okay, I promise."

"So do you want me to pick you up tonight?" Adam asked.

"Nah, I know where the church is. I'll drive myself over there," Danny answered.

"Danny, have you looked into that list of domestic abuse counseling services that I gave you?" Adam asked. "As I've said, I'll be happy to help you get enrolled in one. But I can't make you do it. And Linda can't make you do it. You have to want to help yourself. Just going to church and the AA meetings will be a huge start, but you may need more help than that."

"Well, da—durn it, Preacher," Danny said, "I've agreed to go to church and the AA meetings—now you want me to go to counseling, too?"

For a moment Evelyn was afraid that this was going to be too much change for Danny, but finally he shrugged and pulled Linda closer to him. " You promise to be patient with me and help me?" he asked.

"Hon, you know I've been patient with you a long time, but I promise to be even more patient, and I'll do everything I can to help you."

Adam and Evelyn said their goodbyes, and Linda followed them out onto the porch, where she grabbed Evelyn in a tight hug. "Thank you for standing up to him," she whispered. "Thank y'all for coming by," she said in a normal voice, then headed back inside. She didn't want Danny to think she was standing on the porch talking about him.

"Congratulations!" Adam said after they were back in the car and headed home.

"About what?"

"On your first act as a minister's wife."

"Well, I don't think I handled it like a minister's wife. I was afraid you'd be upset with me for the language I used."

"Sometimes you have to talk to a person in the language they understand before you can get through to them. And besides that, your language was fine. And since I haven't told you lately, I love you."

Evelyn sat in silence. She knew she'd told him that she loved him, but did he expect her to say it back every time he said it?

"I'm waiting," Adam said.

Well, that answered her question. "I love you, too," she mumbled.

"What? I couldn't hear you," Adam said, cupping his hand behind his ear.

Laughter unexpectedly erupted from Evelyn. "I love you, too," she said a little louder.

"Do you have any idea what it does to me to hear you say that?" Adam asked. "I've never been in love with a woman before. Sure, I had my teenage and young man crushes, but that was just puppy love. This is the real thing, and I can't believe I've finally found it. Or that it's found me."

"How do you know it's real?" Evelyn asked. "I thought I loved Darren. Totally believed it was real. And I thought he loved me, too, when we first got married. Then he started acting different. He'd get upset if I didn't wear the clothes he picked out for me to wear to a certain party. Or if he thought I was spending too much time with any particular man. He'd watch me to make sure I was reacting correctly at his functions, and it got so bad that I was in knots by the time we'd get home. But I convinced myself he was just doing it because he loved me. And I kept telling myself that I loved him enough to keep trying.

"But when he started getting really verbally mean, I started waking up to the fact that it wasn't love on his part. And now I'm not sure that I know what real love feels like, even though I told you that I love you. How do you know? How do I know?"

"The more I hear about that jerk, the more I want to slug him," Adam said, and had to take a moment to get his emotions under control before answering Evelyn.

"This is how I know I love you, Eve. I love looking at you. I love hearing your voice, your laugh, and that slight intake of breath when I start to kiss you. I love just sitting in the room with you when we aren't even talking. I love the way you look. I love the way you think. There is nothing about you that I don't love.

"I want to sleep with you every night. Not just to make love, but to know you're there beside me. I want to wake up with you every morning. I want to know that you'll be there every night when I get home.

"That's how I know it's real for me. I guess everybody has to have their own reasons for believing the love they feel is real, because everybody comes into love from their own individual set of circumstances.

"Like you, for instance. You've got to know that I'm not like Darren before you can totally feel free to love me. But I promise you that I'll do everything I can to convince you that I'm nothing like that guy. All I'm asking from you is a lifetime to prove it."

"I know. But I also know that there will be times when I forget and compare you with him, and that's going to hurt you. I don't want to hurt you, but I know I will. What if you lose patience with me and decide I'm not worth your time?"

They had just pulled into the garage at their house, so Adam killed the car and turned to Evelyn.

"All I'm asking is that you try me. Trust me and try me. We can work this out if we both want it to work. Is that asking too much?"

"No. It's asking just enough. I know now that I want it to work, too. I think my problem with you is that you make me have feelings I never had with Darren. Of course we had sex, I have Anna to show for that, but I never cared if we did or not. And that lets me know that we never made love. But you make me want things I never even knew I wanted." Evelyn felt her face start to turn red, and dropped her head.

"What kind of things?" Adam asked, cupping her chin and turning her eyes back to him.

"Adam! I can't just tell you stuff like that."

"Of course you can. That's what husbands and wives are supposed to do. Tell me how I make you feel."

Clearing her voice, Evelyn said, "Well—um—okay. When you get close to me, I want to be closer. I want to feel your arms around me. I want to feel your lips on mine. I want to make love with you.

"And that scares me! What if I'm just feeling lust? I've never felt like this before, and it makes me feel like—well, I'm not sure how it makes me feel, except really good and afraid at the same time!"

Adam took Evelyn's hand and splayed it over his heart. "Feel my heart pounding, Eve? Just hearing you say the words have me so turned on that I'm about to explode! But I told you that you'd have to tell me when you're ready to make love. I won't force you into something you're not ready for.

"And I sure hope you're not about to say it right now, because I have to get dressed for the AA meeting tonight. I can't skip now that Danny may show up."

"Okay, I won't say it right now, but I'm getting really close," Evelyn said, getting quickly out of the car and heading inside.

CHAPTER 18

EVELYN CAME SLOWLY AWAKE, TAKING A MOMENT TO RE-member where she was. Her first thoughts were of Anna. Then she remembered that Anna was still with her mom. She missed her baby so much, and wanted Thanksgiving to hurry and get here.

Then Christmas. What would Christmas with Adam be like? Maybe her mom and Fred could come back here for Christmas. Or—maybe they could just stay from Thanksgiving until Christmas! What a lovely thought. Evelyn smiled at the possibility as she dressed, combed her hair, and put on just the hint of pre-breakfast makeup.

As she walked down the stairway and headed for the kitchen she could hear Adam on his phone. She didn't know whether to go into the kitchen or give him a chance to finish his call, but as she hesitated she heard him sign off. When she entered the kitchen, he was perched on one of the stools that surrounded the breakfast bar.

"Good morning, beautiful!" Adam greeted her. "Would you like some coffee and breakfast?"

"I'll just get some coffee, then maybe eat some toast in a little while."

"Now, you need to nourish that gorgeous body. I don't want it changing. I love it just the way it is."

"Trust me, it doesn't take a lot to keep this body just the way it is," Evelyn assured him, and headed for the coffee pot. But as she walked by Adam, he stood and took her by the shoulders and maneuvered her to a stool.

"You just sit right here and I'll get you some coffee. Are you sure you don't want me to make you some breakfast?" he asked.

"No, I'm good for now, but thanks, anyway. You go ahead and eat if you want to. In fact, I need to be making your breakfast," she said, as an afterthought.

"Why do you need to make my breakfast? I'm perfectly able to make my own breakfast."

"Oh!" Evelyn said quietly.

"What? Have I said the wrong thing?"

"No. It's just that Darren always expected me to make his breakfast. He said that's what wives do."

Adam poured two mugs of coffee and set one down in front of her. Then he sat down and pulled his stool very close, facing her, causing her to almost be sitting between his legs. He rested one arm on the bar in front of her and the other arm on the back of her stool. And just sat and looked at her.

"*Seriously?* Do you honestly expect me to sit here and drink coffee while you perch there and watch me? I feel like a mouse in a field with a hawk perched on a fence post, just waiting to swoop down on me!"

Adam moved the mugs out of reach, wrapped both arms around her and pulled her as close as the stools would let him, then lowered his lips to hers in a kiss that rocked her to her inner soul. Just before she thought she would surely swoon, he pulled away and slid her mug back in front of her.

"I've been fantasizing about starting my day like this since the day I looked up and saw you sitting in the back of the church."

Struggling to get her voice back, Evelyn said, "Okay, now that you have that behind you, you can back up some."

"Nope. You're going to have to get used to me being in your space. I'm not happy being any farther away from you than right where I am."

"You're impossible!" Evelyn said, and attempted to scoot her stool away from him. But he immediately caught the legs of the stool with the toes of his shoes and kept her close.

"I thought you enjoyed being close to me," Adam said.

"That's the problem! I like it too much. I can't think straight when you're this close."

"Good," Adam said, and pulled his stool a little closer. "Now, I need to talk with you about a couple of things."

"Uh-oh," Evelyn muttered.

"First," Adam continued as if he hadn't heard her, "I don't have a fixed breakfast routine. So you don't even need to think about it. We can decide what we're going to do when we get up. Okay?"

"Okay."

"The second thing is that some of the ladies at church want to give us a reception party. They said that since we cheated them out of going to our wedding, it's the least we can do for them. Is that okay?"

"Do I have a choice?" Evelyn asked, old feelings of resentment springing into her before she could stop them. When Darren informed her of an upcoming party or event, he announced that it was happening and she was expected to act accordingly.

Adam had seen her expression change and the anger in her eyes even before she spoke. And he knew exactly where it was coming from.

He cupped her chin and pulled her face to look at him. "Eve, you always have a choice where I'm concerned. I don't know how many times I'll need to tell you this, but I will keep saying it until you're convinced. I told the ladies that I would ask you about it and we would go with whatever you decided."

"You told them that? That I would make the decision?" Disbelief sounded in Evelyn's voice. When she'd left Darren and rediscovered the freedom of making her own decisions, she'd promised herself that she would never again give someone else that power over her. That's one of the reasons she'd been so reluctant to marry Adam and get back into that kind of situation. But could it be possible that Adam really was as different from Darren as it seemed?

"Eve, as husband and wife, we're supposed to be partners. The first Eve was made from one of Adam's ribs when God created male and female. His rib, Eve. That means she belongs by his side. Not in front of or behind him. Beside him. Helping him make the right decisions. Making those decisions together. It is not my place, as your husband, to take away your choices, or to make you less of a person just because you're a wife—a woman."

Evelyn turned to face Adam, which put her knees directly between his legs, in a most intimate position. Then she placed her hands on each side of his face, pulled him close, and softly kissed him on the lips. But before he could react and claim more, she pulled back. "I'm beginning to believe I'm going to enjoy being Mrs. Adam Singletary," she said.

"You ain't seen nothing, yet," Adam said, twitching his eyebrows up and down. "Now, since we can't get serious with doing what's uppermost in my mind, I'm going to put these mugs in the dishwasher, then call the ladies and tell them that you've given the okay on the reception."

"Did Danny show up last night?" Evelyn asked, standing and rinsing the mugs out and handing them to Adam to put in the dishwasher. It felt right. Just that small chore, done together, felt so right to her.

"Yes! He was early, and so was Ron, and they seemed to reconnect as if it had only been yesterday since they were friends. I've really got my hopes up that this will encourage Danny to get back to church like he promised Linda he would.

"Okay, let me run to my office where my Rolodex is and call the ladies," Adam said, and gave Evelyn a quick kiss before heading up the stairs.

Not knowing what to do with herself, Evelyn made her way to the library, and sat down with the same book that she'd planned to read yesterday.

She glanced out the window and realized the sun was shining. The rain from yesterday had knocked a lot of leaves off the trees, and she could imagine Anna and Mangy running and jumping in the leaves. She'd ask Adam if they could get the person who took care of the yard to leave some leaves on the ground until after Thanksgiving. One of her favorite childhood memories was playing in the leaves with friends.

She was smiling at the memory when Adam appeared at the door.

"The police department called. They've captured Darren and his friend. They have them in jail, and want us to come down and identify them to make sure they're the same two people we saw and heard at Cracker Barrel."

CHAPTER 19

DREAD CLUTCHED EVELYN AT THE THOUGHT OF WHAT DARren might try, now that he'd been found out and actually arrested. Of course he would blame it all on Evelyn. What kind of revenge would he plan if he had to spend time in jail? Would he try to harm her or Anna?

"What?" Adam asked, watching the emotions play across Evelyn's face.

"I'm really afraid of him, now that he's been backed into a corner. I've seen him react very badly, a lot worse than he ever did with me, when people would deny him what he wanted. I've seen him get physical a few times.

"I'm really afraid that he may try to harm Anna just to get back at me. He knows nothing about playing fairly.

"I can't believe this is happening! I had believed that once I got to Nashville and settled in, he'd forget about me and not try to find me. And I was hoping that he couldn't find me, even if he tried. I guess I just didn't know how determined and spiteful he was."

"Eve, you're not in this alone anymore. What he does to you, he has to get through me to do. Together, we can beat him at his own game."

"I hope you're right," Evelyn said, getting up to get her purse so they could go to the police department and get it over with.

IT DIDN'T TAKE Adam and Evelyn long to arrive at the Criminal Justice Center in downtown Nashville, where Darren and his hired hand were being held.

But apparently communications had failed, because when Adam and Evelyn walked into the CJC and to the desk where Detective Greer had instructed Adam to meet him, the first thing they saw was Darren collecting his personal items.

As they stopped to stare at Darren's back, Detective Greer stepped up to them. "I don't know what happened, but he made bail before I got here. His sidekick is still being held."

"Oh, I'm sure of what happened," Evelyn said. "He called his hotshot lawyer in Meridian and told them he was innocent and the lawyer probably made dire threats as to what he could do or have done, legally, if Darren wasn't released. That guy is what gives lawyers a bad name. Trust me, I've had dealings with him."

Just then Darren turned and spotted Evelyn and started toward them. "You fat bitch! You're trying to destroy me, but I'll show you who's in charge. You'll wish you were dead before I'm done with you!" With a snort of contempt he reached for Evelyn, but collided with Adam's balled up fist and fell to the floor, seemingly knocked out cold.

Instantly a police officer was on the scene. "What's going on here?" he asked.

"Officer," Adam said, "We have witnesses that this man threatened my wife's life. If he's allowed to go free, I'm afraid for her safety. He needs to be back behind bars."

"He's right," Detective Greer said. "I was standing right here and saw the entire thing."

Darren was arrested for the second time that day and placed back in a cell, charged with assault. He hadn't made any more threats to Evelyn, but loathing glared from his eyes every time he had a chance to look at her.

Evelyn had witnessed his intimidation antics before, and recognized them for what they were.

After she and Adam had filed charges against Darren and got a restraining order to keep him away from Evelyn, Anna, Adam, and any property they had, they left the Criminal Justice Center and headed home.

"How does your hand feel?" Evelyn asked.

Adam held out his red and swollen knuckles on his right hand for her to see. "Probably better than his jaw," he answered.

Suddenly Evelyn's brain did a perfect photo flash of Darren coming at her and the look on his face when Adam's fist connected with his jaw, and she couldn't retain the laughter that erupted from her.

Almost instantly, Adam joined her.

After they had worn themselves down and felt the tension draining from their bodies, Evelyn said, "You have no idea how many times I fantasized about doing what you did to him. And the look of disbelief on his face was just priceless! I'll think of that every time I think of the despicable things he said to Anna and me, and I'll feel better."

"As a minister, here's where I should warn you that 'vengeance is the Lord's,' but maybe what you saw was the Lord's vengeance displayed just for you. So I say go ahead and enjoy the moment."

"Do you need to go to the doctor with your hand?"

"Nah. I'll put ice on it when we get home, and it'll be fine."

"I would kiss it and make it better, but I'm afraid your hand may still have some of Darren's skin particles on it, and I don't want to contaminate my lips with anything about him."

"Hmm. I need to remind myself not to ever make an enemy of you! You can be downright mean when you want to be. But you can kiss my lips and make me feel better all over."

"Well, since you're driving, I guess I'd better pass on that," Evelyn said, feeling her heart jump a few beats.

"Coward," was all Adam said.

They drove the rest of the way home in silence, but once they got home and had walked inside the house, Adam took Evelyn's arm and turned her toward him. "I'm not driving now."

The fire in his eyes weakened Evelyn's legs to the point that she almost staggered as Adam pulled her close to him, not quite touching, and just watched her.

"Oh, so now you want me to follow through with your suggestion in the car?"

"That's precisely what I want."

So Evelyn took his left hand and kissed the knuckles before saying, "We'll just pretend that this is the hand that was hurt."

"Nope, that's not what I suggested in the car."

"Adam—" Suddenly the huge, empty house loomed around Evelyn, and her heart was pounding out of her chest. She was sure Adam could see her clothes vibrating with the thumps of her heart.

She lifted her mouth and gently touched his, but stepped back when he tried to claim her lips. "I want to thank you for standing up for me like you did. I've never felt like the protected damsel in distress before."

When Adam started to respond, she said, "Shhhh," and placed another light kiss on the left corner of his mouth, again stepping back just out of his reach.

"And I want to thank you for helping me fill out all those forms for the restraining order. I'm happy that we did that, although I don't know if it will work or not."

This time she kissed the right corner of his mouth. She could tell Adam's face was becoming flushed and he was having a hard time containing himself, and a feeling of power went through her that she'd never felt before.

She really could be a seductress with the right man, she realized. Darren had never let her take the lead in their sex acts, or any other area of their life, so she wasn't sure if she would like it or not. But she knew now that she liked it. She liked it a lot.

"Adam?" she whispered, just close enough that her lips weren't touching his, but her breath caressed his lips in a sensual breeze.

"Yes?" he answered, wondering how he managed to even get that through his throat, which seemed to be closing in on him.

"Do you think you could make love with me, even with your hurt hand and swollen knuckles?"

CHAPTER 20

EVELYN CAME SLOWLY AWAKE TO QUIET BREATHING NEXT to her. At first she thought Anna had crawled into bed with her. Then she remembered that Anna was still in Mississippi with her mom.

She became aware of Adam's arm circling her waist as they lay spooned together—and then she remembered the night before. She and Adam had made love several times, and each time had been slower and gentler than the time before. She never knew a man could be so caring and tender.

For the first time in her life, Evelyn could see her future. She could imagine growing old with Adam. She could imagine having his children and filling this house full of love and laughter. And she could imagine growing old and gray and being content to sit on the porch and rock the days away.

Her musings came to a screeching halt. No. Never could she imagine Adam Singletary sitting on the porch and rocking the days away. Maybe sitting and rocking for a little while, but he'd be up with his cane and busy with something. That thought brought a chuckle from her.

"Are you awake, my beloved, or are you laughing in your sleep?" Adam's voice, gravelly from just waking up, was close to her ear.

"I'm awake," Evelyn murmured, too shy to turn and look at Adam in the light of the new day.

She'd had no idea that she was a woman of so much passion. But with him she'd felt free to be herself and enjoy making love. He'd constantly complimented her and used words of such great endearment that she couldn't help but react like a woman full of love.

"Are you ready for me to make you some breakfast?" he asked. "I'd rather stay right here and continue what we kind of started last night, but I have a good bit of work to do today."

"Kind of started?" Evelyn asked as she turned to him, her shyness completely gone at his reference to the night they'd just spent.

A laugh rolled from Adam as he bent to capture her lips in his. "I thought that might get your attention.

"Incidentally, you are one remarkable woman! I'm sure I'll never get tired of being with you. In the bed, or anywhere else. You're always a surprise, and I love it! And I'll love you forever."

He kissed her again, then sprang from the bed. "This is me fleeing from temptation. If I stay beside you one more minute, I'll be lost in those beautiful eyes of yours. I'll go downstairs and start breakfast, if you want to jump in the shower."

Evelyn lay for another moment, soaking in the experience. Never, after all the cruel words that Darren had said to her, could she have ever dreamed she'd find someone like Adam who relished her body.

But not just her body. Adam seemed to enjoy just being with her, so she knew he loved her personality and mental capabilities, as well.

Evelyn raised her arms over her head in a relaxed, luxurious stretch, then, letting out a giggle, went to the bathroom to get a shower.

After showering and dressing, she headed downstairs toward

the wonderful scents of coffee and bacon and eggs. She could get used to this, she thought.

When she got to the kitchen door, Evelyn stopped and took in the scene. Adam had a small TV tuned to a local station and was watching the morning news while he made breakfast. His back was to her, and he hadn't heard her come down the stairs. She quietly made her way to him and put her arms around his waist.

"Something sure smells delicious," she said, snuggling into him.

Adam's entire body went totally still. Had she done something wrong? Evelyn wondered, feeling a little panicky.

"So this is what it's like to wake up in the morning with the woman you love," he said, turning and taking her in his arms. "It feels like I've been waiting for this moment my entire life. How could Darren let someone as loving as you are get away from him?"

"Because Darren never allowed me to show my love," Evelyn whispered. "He had to be the one in charge. The one who made all the advances. I was never allowed to open up and be who I wanted to be. I knew there was a wanton woman deep inside me, but you're the only person who has ever opened the cage and let her out."

"Oh, my! Are you saying that I'm just getting a glimpse of the woman you really are?"

"I'm afraid that's the case," Evelyn answered, with a gleam in her eyes. "So you should be afraid. Very afraid."

"Now here's a story we don't get very often," the TV announcer said. "The minister of Grace For All Church, Adam Singletary, coldcocked his wife's ex-husband down at the Criminal Justice Center yesterday. It seems that the ex acted menacingly toward the pastor's wife, and the pastor took offense. We'll keep you up on this story as we learn more."

You could hear the other people in the television station

laughing and talking as they faded to a commercial.

Adam went to the TV and switched it off, then turned back to Evelyn. "Let's eat this breakfast before it gets cold," he said, as if he hadn't heard the news report.

"Aren't you upset?" Evelyn questioned.

"Why? It is what it is. I did it, and somehow the news got wind of it, so there's no need to be upset."

"Adam, what if I've caused you to lose your job?"

"Lose my job? No, I don't think that'll happen. What it may do is fill more seats at the church tomorrow. I'll just bet there'll be a larger crowd for two reasons. One will be to see my new wife, so more of the congregation who don't come on a regular basis will probably show up. And two, we'll probably get some looky loos who want to see the minister who fights like a street brawler."

At this, Adam tilted his head back and laughed. "You know, that sounded really funny coming over the TV. Now, here, take this plate and get some of this omelet, which I hope you like, and here's some toast and bacon. Sit and start eating, and I'll bring us some coffee."

Evelyn glanced at Adam's knuckles. They were still bruised and swollen. "Does your hand hurt?"

"Only when I move it. But it'll be fine in a few days. I'm not a stranger to this. I was in boxing class when I was in high school. Plus, I was a typical teenage guy. There were fights that broke out. Don't get me wrong. I wasn't a street brawler, but I didn't necessarily run from a fight, either."

After yesterday, Evelyn didn't have any problem picturing him in the role he'd just described.

They were barely finished with the meal when the phone started ringing. Adam answered it, and Evelyn could tell he was getting a kick out of the story he was being questioned about.

Soon Evelyn heard her cell phone start ringing upstairs. She hurried to get the call and answered just before voice mail kicked in. "Hello? This is Eve."

"Eve! Are you okay?" Julie asked, concern sounding in her voice.

"You must have just seen the television report," Evelyn said. "Yes, I'm fine. Darren didn't touch me, but I think he was thinking about it just before he ran into Adam's fist."

"Has he ever hit you before?"

"No, but there were a few times that I was sure he wanted to."

Suddenly Julie went into a peal of laughter. "I've always loved Pastor Adam because he seemed so *real!* But, even at that, I can't believe he actually hit someone!" And she laughed again.

"He did a good job, too, because his knuckles are still bruised and swollen this morning."

"Are you nervous about being at church and the reception, tomorrow?"

"I haven't had much time to think about tomorrow, but, yes, I'm a little nervous of how everyone is going to react to me, and me to them, actually. I never even had a chance to answer all of those messages I had gotten before everything burned up." She silently wondered when she would hear from the insurance company, and if Darren would have to spend jail time.

"I'm so sorry about that," Julie said. "I almost felt responsible for it, since I was in charge and you were out of town when it happened. Jim finally convinced me that I didn't have any way of knowing it would happen."

"Of course you didn't know. But I've been meaning to ask you if anyone had come into the store acting weird before the fire happened?"

"There was a man who came in the day before it happened. He was asking me if I was the owner, and when I said that I wasn't, he wanted to know who was. I told him your name, because I thought he was some kind of salesman, but he just kind of smiled when I told him you were the owner. Then he wandered around a little bit mumbling to himself before he left.

"I thought he was a little weird, but didn't think about him again until you just asked."

"Do you remember what he looked like?"

"He was medium height and build, and I think his hair was light brown or dark blond. Oh! He had strange, glistening blue eyes. Almost like he was possessed."

"That was Darren," Evelyn said. "No doubt about that description. Can you remember anything else he said?"

"When he was wandering around, I thought he mentioned something about this trash should be burned."

"Did you tell the police about this?"

"No. They didn't ask me about a person. They just asked me where I was the night it happened. Like I was there in the middle of the night and knew why the fire started!" Indignation was loud and clear in Julie's voice.

"At the time, they still didn't know if it was arson or an accident. They'll probably question you now that they know it was arson and who was responsible."

"Well, I think I'll call them Monday and tell them about Darren being in the store."

"I hate to drag you into this more than you already are, but anything you can tell them will help," Evelyn said.

"Okay. I need to go, but I want you to know that I'll be watching out for you tomorrow. If I see you standing alone looking lost, I'll run to your rescue. And if I don't see you and you need me, just look for me. I've got your back."

Tears filled Evelyn's eyes. It really was good to have a friend. "Thanks, Julie. I feel better just knowing that I can count on you."

CHAPTER 21

"**A**RE YOU NERVOUS?" ADAM ASKED AS HE DROVE THEM to church.

"Yes. I have about a million butterflies in my stomach."

"I promise not to leave you stranded, so try to relax. I'll be right by your side to run interference if anyone gets too personal with you. You're going to be fine. They'll love you, just like I love you.

"And you look beautiful. I love what that mint green dress does to your eyes. It's like they can't decide if they want to be green, golden or yellow."

Adam pulled into the parking lot of the church and came to a stop. "Would you look at this?" he said in awe. "You've filled more parking spaces at this church than I ever have!"

"Me? I'm not the one who coldcocked someone at the jail house and wound up in the morning news. I think you're the one they want to see."

"But you're at the bottom of it all. It was *your* ex-husband that I hit. It was *your* store that was burned to the ground. And it's *your* fault that I couldn't resist loving you and marrying you and wanted to spend the rest of my life with you. So, see, it's all *your* fault!"

Before Evelyn could answer, Adam had proceeded to his reserved parking spot. "Now let's go in and see if all the seats are taken. I really hope they are."

Evelyn felt conspicuous as Adam led her in through a side door and straight into the front of the auditorium. Hundreds of people who had been standing and visiting with each other slowly quieted, and all heads turned to look at Adam and Evelyn.

Thankfully, at that point the song leader walked to the microphone and said, "Good morning! How wonderful to see so many people here this morning. If you'll all begin to take your seats, we'll get started in about five minutes.

"Now, don't worry! You'll all have a chance to talk with the newlyweds at the reception directly following the service."

After Adam and Evelyn sat down on the first row and the singing started, Evelyn began to relax a little. But after directing several songs, the song leader said, "Okay, folks, Pastor Adam would like to introduce you to his new bride. Pastor, if you and your wife will come up on stage so everyone can get a better look, I'll turn the microphone over to you."

"Oh, dear!" Evelyn murmured.

"Don't back down on me now," Adam whispered in her ear, and took her hand and stood up. He held on to her hand as they climbed the five steps to the stage.

Adam shook the song leader's hand and stepped to the mic, still holding on to Evelyn's hand.

"I know this is very sudden to you all, and I know that most of you don't or didn't know Evelyn Carmichael existed until a week ago when our wedding was announced. But I've known she existed for years. I just didn't know where she was or what her name was.

"But a couple of months ago she eased quietly in the back door of this building and sat down in the very back row, and when I saw her, I knew the person that I carried in my heart had just walked into my life.

"We apologize for getting married so quickly, without letting you all be a part of the ceremony, but there were reasons that I won't go into right now that led us to our hasty wedding. And, no—it wasn't a shotgun wedding!"

Laughter and applause caused Adam to pause for a few moments before continuing.

"A lot of you have tried to hook me up with someone you know, and I really did and do appreciate your concern for me. And some of you had begun to be kind of doubtful that I'd ever find someone I wanted to share my life with.

"So let me assure you that I have met that person. And to make it even more perfect, her name is Eve. Well, her name is Evelyn, but for me, she's my Eve.

"You'll never know how much pleasure it gives me to introduce you to my wife, Evelyn Nicole Singletary."

To Evelyn's surprise, the auditorium erupted in applause and the people came to their feet in what seemed to be a genuine welcome. When everyone had sat down, Adam continued, "Eve has a beautiful four-year-old daughter you're all going to love. Annabel is her name. She's with her grandmother, Eve's mom, in Mississippi, now, but will be home for Thanksgiving.

"We'll talk more at the reception, which we both thank all of you for putting together."

Back in their seats, Adam put his arm on the back of Evelyn's chair and whispered, "See, I told you they'd love you."

Evelyn smiled up at him, and thought *I hope you're right.*

As the interim minister preached, Evelyn thought back to the first time she'd walked into this building and sat down in that back row. A lot had happened between that back row and the front row where she sat now.

She had no doubt that she loved Adam Singletary or that he loved her. And she had no doubt that he would be a good husband and a wonderful dad to Anna. She did, however, still have some worries about how she'd fit in with this congregation as a minister's wife.

As if sensing her thoughts, Adam took her hand and gave it a tight squeeze, as if to reassure her that together they could weather any storm they faced. And just like that, all her doubts were dissolved. A smile crept across her face as she looked up at him.

Leaning down, Adam placed a quick, light kiss on her lips, right there on the front row of the church, in front of God and all the congregation.

ABOUT THE AUTHOR

P AT BALLARD LIVES IN NASHVILLE, TN. SHE WRITES MOTI-vational romance novels to show that plus-size women can be just as sexy, romantic and exciting as their slim sisters. Visit Pat on the web at http://www.patballard.com.

LOOK FOR HER OTHER BOOKS published by Pearlsong Press— *Dangerous Curves Ahead: Short Stories, Wanted: One Groom, Nobody's Perfect, His Brother's Child, A Worthy Heir, Abigail's Revenge, The Best Man, Dangerous Love* & the novella *ASAP Nanny*—in trade paperback or ebook at your favorite online bookstore, as well as at www.pearlsong.com.

The Queen of Rubenesque Romances has also ventured into nonfiction! *10 Steps to Loving Your Body (No Matter What Size You Are)* has been called "your body's best friend in pocket form" and has been named one of the Top 100 Best Self-Help Books of All Time by Self-help.fm. Her free ebook *Something to Think About: Reflections on Life, Family, Body Image & Other Weighty Matters by the Queen of Rubenesque Romances* can be downloaded from the Pearlsong Press website.

ABOUT PEARLSONG PRESS

PEARLSONG PRESS IS AN INDEPENDENT PUBLISHING COMpany dedicated to providing books and resources that entertain while expanding perspectives on the self and the world. The company was founded by Peggy Elam, Ph.D., a psychologist and journalist, in 2003.

We encourage you to enjoy other Pearlsong Press books, which you can purchase at www.pearlsong.com or your favorite bookstore. Keep up with us through our blog at www.pearlsongpress.com as we promote health and happiness at every size.

ROMANCE FEATURING BIG BEAUTIFUL HEROINES

by Pat Ballard, the Queen of Rubenesque Romances:
ASAP Nanny | *Dangerous Love* | *The Best Man* | *Abigail's Revenge*
Dangerous Curves Ahead: Short Stories | *Wanted: One Groom*
Nobody's Perfect | *His Brother's Child* | *A Worthy Heir*
by Rebecca Brock | *The Giving Season*
& by Judy Bagshaw | *Kiss Me, Nate!* & *At Long Last, Love*

OTHER FICTION & NONFICTION

10 Steps to Loving Your Body (No Matter What Size You Are)
by Pat Ballard

Soul Mothers' Wisdom: Seven Insights for the Single Mother
by Bette J. Freedson

Heretics: A Love Story & *The Singing of Swans* by Mary Saracino

Judith & *Love is the Thread: A Knitting Friendship* by Leslie Moïse

Fatropolis by Tracey L. Thompson

*The Falstaff Vampire Files, Bride of the Living Dead, Larger Than
Death, Large Target, At Large* & *A Ton of Trouble* by Lynne Murray

The Season of Lost Children by Karen Blomain

Fallen Embers & *Blowing Embers* by Lauri J Owen

The Program & *The Fat Lady Sings* by Charlie Lovett

Syd Arthur & *Beyond Measure: A Memoir About Short Stature &
Inner Growth* by Ellen Frankel

Measure By Measure by Rebecca Fox & William Sherman

FatLand & *FatLand: The Early Days*—Books 1 & 2 of The
FatLand Trilogy by Frannie Zellman

Fat Poets Speak: Voices of the Fat Poets' Society & *Fat Poets Speak 2:
Living and Loving Fatly* edited by Frannie Zellman

Acceptable Prejudice? Fat, Rhetoric & Social Justice &
Talking Fat: Health vs. Persuasion in the War on Our Bodies
by Lonie McMichael, Ph.D.

Hiking the Pack Line: Moving from Grief to a Joyful Life
by Bonnie Shapbell

A Life Interrupted: Living with Brain Injury by Louise Mathewson

ExtraOrdinary: An End of Life Story Without End
by Michele Tamaren & Michael Wittner

*Taking Up Space: How Eating Well & Exercising Regularly Changed
My Life* by Pattie Thomas, Ph.D. with Carl Wilkerson, M.B.A.
(foreword by Paul Campos, author of *The Obesity Myth*)

*Off Kilter: A Woman's Journey to Peace with Scoliosis, Her
Mother & Her Polish Heritage* by Linda C. Wisniewski

Unconventional Means: The Dream Down Under
by Anne Richardson Williams

Splendid Seniors: Great Lives, Great Deeds by Jack Adler